To Ben Hollingsworth —
Hope U enjoy!
Sterling Quinlan

SOMETHING IN BETWEEN

SOMETHING IN BETWEEN

a novel

Sterling Quinlan

GEORGE BRAZILLER   NEW YORK

First published in the United States in 1994 by
George Braziller, Inc.

For information, please write to the publisher:
George Braziller, Inc.
60 Madison Avenue
New York, New York 10010

Library of Congress Cataloging-in-Publication Data:
Quinlan, Sterling.
Something in Between / Sterling Quinlan
        p.   cm.
    ISBN 0-8076-1364-9
    I.   Title
PS3567.U337S65   1994   94-16295
813'.54—dc   CIP

Book design by Lundquist Design

Printed and bound in the United States

First Edition

To Mary and Stuart

It seems gothic now, but there was a dream back then.

It came at a time when it was difficult to dream. The time was the thirties and there was a Depression that spared only a few. But because America was young, still strong in spirit, the dream went blithely on.

The Great American Dream some called it. Others called it by other names, but everyone agreed that it was a good dream. And that in having it, America was uniquely blessed.

And so the dream was born. Some say it was unborn. But that is wrong. It truly was born.

Some say it was a wrong dream, or a dream that went wrong. That it never could have worked. Or that being a good dream, it had to go wrong because all dreams are nonsense.

Others called it *The Stillborn Dream*. Maybe that is closer to the truth.

But whatever one chooses to call it, no matter how one looks back upon it, the dream should be reexamined.

The mood of the country today, it is fair to say, is mean-spirited, angry, hostile. How was it back then? Is there a present-day corollary? Is there something to be gained by looking back, comparing that era with this one ?

One thing is sure: It was, in a sense, a mythic time when the Dream was building. Keltnor knows because he was there. Life is a profoundly personal journey filled with secrets we would prefer others not know. Ask Keltnor. He saw it all. And it did happen.

The Sick Wife

Mornings were usually pandemonium in the Frank Genesyk house, but Monday mornings were the worst because of Papa Genesyk's giant-sized hangovers. He would pour half a dozen aspirin into his fist, toss them down without water, and blow his nose into the toilet while the sink was filling with cold water. When the sink was full he would plunge his head in and hold it there till his lungs were ready to burst. At last, he'd pull out, spluttering, shaking his head like an angry dog, and roar, "Goddamn!" three times, very rapidly.

Downstairs, Mama Genesyk and the two girls paid no attention except to exchange glances and promise themselves to stay out of Papa's way.

Frank Genesyk did not believe in doing things by half measures. He began drinking early every Saturday afternoon, and because he was a man of determination, he was glassy-eyed by supper time. He remained that way all night, taking only a few hours for sleep, and on Sunday morning he was at it again. At approximately seven o'clock that night, his head would collapse on the table next to a bottle of whiskey and a stein of beer.

That ended the weekend.

The next morning Frank Genesyk would try to shake his hangover with the same determination he applied to getting drunk. "Oh Goddamn!" he yelled again and blew his nose into the toilet once more.

He heard his daughters laughing at him from down-stairs. One said in Lithuanian, not for his benefit really, but for her own amusement: "Take it easy, Pa."

Can't speak Lithuanian worth a shit, he thought. Only time they used the *proper* language was when they knew his mood was bad and they wanted to please him. His daughters were a source of frustration to him. He no longer felt he understood them. And he was certain they did not understand him. He often had the feeling that they were laughing at him. Sometimes he would catch them smirking, or smiling. "What's so funny?" he'd ask.

One would reply: "Oh Pa, you're just funny, that's all."

Funny was he? He'd give them "funny." Spoiled teenaged high school kids with ants in their pants was what they were. Boys hanging around with their zippers loose. Four of them in the kitchen last night making remarks about him while the girls popped corn. What was this damn world coming to? he asked himself. Goddamn radio gave kids crazy ideas. If things were this bad in 1933, what would it be like a few years from now?

Frank Genesyk tried to prepare himself for another uneventful week. Plus the ordeal of getting the booze out of his system. No drinking during the week, except a few beers maybe. The day shift at South Chicago Steel Mills. He had nothing to be ashamed of. Let the girls laugh all they wanted. After all, he was a man of property. He had standing. A six-room brick bungalow on the east side of Lake Calumet was nothing to be sneezed at. Nine thousand dollars it cost! Already, after ten years, thirty-five hundred had been paid off. And he was still working! Unbelievably lucky. Half the workers in the plant gone. His two daughters didn't even know there was a Depression going on. Gets much worse, maybe he'd go back to the Old Country.

But thank God he had a fat wife of congenial disposition. One who worked hard and never complained. Yes, he thought with a measure of pride, not once could he ever remember Sophie complaining. Nothing like stock from the Old Country. And she spoke the *proper* language most of the time and did not share the girls' modern ways, although on this point he sometimes had his doubts.

He heard Sophie call out to their eighteen-year-old: "Dorothy, go by the store quick. We're outta butter."

"How can I?" Dorothy said. "I ain't dressed yet and Pa's still in the bathroom."

"Jesus!" Papa Genesyk muttered. *If I was down there and kicked her plump little ass, she'd find a way to go to the store.*

"Make him get out of the bathroom," said Mary, their younger one.

"Not me. *You* try."

Only fourteen, Mary's figure was developing nicely. Too nicely, thought Papa Genesyk. On weekends, when drunk, a strange look of mischief sometimes came into his eyes. "Ho ho, what's here for me? Pretty soon you give somebody good time, no? Maybe old man try it out first."

"Pa! Don't be disgusting!" Mary would cry and blush.

"Listen, if I ever catch you with a Polack, I'll do it!"

And then, if the mood suited him, he would chase her through the house while Mama Genesyk sat in the kitchen, laughing. She knew her husband couldn't do anything when he was drunk.

Papa Genesyk glanced in the mirror at his swollen, bloodshot eyes, cursed devoutly, and went downstairs.

Dorothy took one look at him and laughed. "I got no

sympathy for you, Pa."

"Who need sympathy?" he growled.

"It's your own fault. You get drunk like a pig every Sunday. Your white suit is a mess. It's a wonder you don't kill yourself."

Frank glared at his oldest and wondered if he should do something about such impertinence. A crack across the face maybe.

"Who feels bad? Not me. Where's my old woman?"

"Ma's in bed."

"In . . . what?"

"She don't feel good. Leave her alone."

"Whatsamatter her?"

"She's sick."

Sick! Papa Genesyk pondered this strange notion. Seldom had the word been uttered in this house except years ago when the girls had their tonsils out. *His old woman of all people!* Suddenly he caught the joke of it and laughed. "Ho ho, she gonna be like the Sick Wife, no?"

Dorothy ignored this comparison with the young wife next door who was frail, consumptive, and had been ailing for two years. Everyone in the neighborhood called her the Sick Wife. Everyone felt sorry for the husband who had to pay the doctor bills, and so much money for medicine.

"So that's it," Papa Genesyk cried, slapping the side of his head. "Tell her we already got one sick wife and to get outta bed!"

"Ma hurts in the stomach," called Mary from the next room where she was admiring how tightly her blouse fit. "There's something wrong with her."

Papa Genesyk made a noise like he was blowing his nose. "Naa! Bellyaches, at's all."

"No, Pa. No bellyache," said Dorothy. "She hurts bad. She needs a doctor."

"Doctor no come this house. He do, I kick him in the ass," said Papa in the proper language.

Dorothy became indignant. "You're old-fashioned, Pa. Doctors are good for people."

"Not my family. Not this house."

"Ma works too hard," chimed Mary, suddenly angered by the realization of how old-fashioned her parents were— both of them, but especially her father. Thank God her life wouldn't be like that.

Papa Genesyk screwed up his face until it was a comical sight. This had to be a joke. And he could go along with it. In fact, he sometimes enjoyed playing the clown when jokes were involved.

"Who works hard if not me? You ever see Frank Genesyk get sick? Hell no! He works. Works. Never get sick. Bring the money. Buy the food. That's all."

He strode into the bedroom where Sophie Genesyk was laying with a bewildered expression on her face. She had heard the conversation, of course, and tried to apologize with her eyes for the shame she felt. Papa looked at her with cold disdain. What kind of foolishness came over a woman to suddenly give herself the idea she could be sick, when she should be at the stove?

"Whatsamatter you?" Sophie had no answer, which only added to his disgust and contempt.

"I hurt here," she finally said, pointing to her stomach.

Papa stared at the region with clinical interest, almost with a trace of sympathy. Then he burst out: "Naa! Only bellyache." And certainly a bellyache was better than a game leg that kept one from walking.

"Eat too much," he said. "You too fat."

Mama Genesyk smiled apologetically. She rubbed her blunt, thick nose with its mole near the top. "I be all right," she said. "I take it easy little while."

"Take it easy?" Papa cried. "To hell with take-it-easy. Thatsa trouble with people today. Too much take-it-easy. Frank Genesyk, he don't take it easy. He don't get sick. No time get sick. You eat too much. Bellyaches, thatsall."

Papa stomped out to the kitchen to get the steaming cup of black coffee that Dorothy had just poured. With it, he took his usual four slices of black rye—kept standing for two days to "get the softness out"—and a pot of honey. He sat there staring straight ahead as though trying to fathom this sudden dislocation in his life.

"Where's the butter?"

"Mary went to the store to get some."

He gave Dorothy a pained expression. If Sophie were up, there would be butter on the table!

Mary returned in a few minutes from the corner grocery. She burst in breathless and shivering from the fifteen-degree cold, set the butter on the table along with a bag filled with the kind of breakfast she and her sister enjoyed: bismarks filled with jelly, sweet rolls, and doughy longjohns. Papa glanced scornfully at this soft, tooth-decaying mess—another sign of the times. This was the generation that was going to take over America, make the country a better place to live? *Aaah*, he grunted. What a hell of a way to start the week.

"I just heard some news," Mary announced. She stopped suddenly, glanced toward the bedroom next to the kitchen. Her voice lowered as though, for some reason, it would be wrong for her mother to hear. "The Sick Wife . . ."

she murmured. "The Sick Wife is worse."

"What's wrong?" asked Dorothy.

"She's very bad."

Dorothy shook her head slowly and glanced toward her father, hoping he would not begin one of his tirades. The Sick Wife had almost become a taboo subject in this house, and only Papa could joke about her.

Stanley Krystosik's wife had come to America only four years ago from Latvia. Two years ago she had married her sturdy, solemn-looking husband who worked at the mills as a puddler. From the very first day of their marriage, it seemed, she had been a burden to her husband. Everything had been tried. Not only doctors, but magic charms, herbs, potions . . . all the cures that the neighborhood women, with their Old World superstitions, could conjure. But each month the Sick Wife grew paler, more listless.

Papa Genesyk was unable to contain himself any longer. "It's no good," he burst out.

"What's no good, Pa?"

"All this nonsense. Where does it lead."

"What nonsense . . . ?"

"People shouldn't be sick so long. Either get better, or . . ."

The girls disagreed simultaneously—and violently. Papa told them to shut up. After all, what did they know about the world? Soon the room was ringing with shouts and insults. Papa began cursing, and said that for all he could tell, maybe his old woman was trying to imitate the Sick Wife. And why not? It must be a great feeling to lay in bed all morning. This is what came of all these modern ideas and modern education. If he had it to do over again, he would never permit his daughters to enter high school.

It was the usual kind of outburst. No better, no worse than others. Nobody ever won. Nobody lost. And, strangely enough, the bitterness disappeared as soon as the argument was over.

Papa Genesyk, to show that he harbored no ill feelings, tossed out his favorite humorous warning as he arose from the table: "As long as you stay away from Polacks."

He said it because he knew how much it irritated both girls. Not that Papa felt the grudge as deeply as he used to. As long as he didn't have to live next door to them. As long as he could live in an area mostly populated by Litvaks. But even that sense of security of living with one's own kind was beginning to change. Two Czech families had moved into the neighborhood recently. And on the next block, there lived a Hungarian family. Young Stanley Krystosik next door—Frank called him "Stash"—was part Lithuanian, part Ukrainian, which was all right as far as Frank was concerned. But he suspected that Stash had a trace of Polish in him—how else would he know all those Polish words?

The girls had grown to like the Poles. The high school football team had several Polish regulars. They were tall, straight, and well mannered. Felix Szakach, their all-state guard, was Polish, and all the girls idolized him. They not only refused to take Papa's bait this time, but Dorothy got in a dig of her own. "What would you do if I married one?"

Papa shrugged. He was not going to bite. Besides, it was time to go to work. "One of us would have to go back to the Old Country," he muttered.

"It wouldn't be me," said Dorothy.

"Me either," Mary taunted.

Dorothy handed him his dinner pail and Thermos bottle. Papa took it, put on his black leather jacket and cap, and left the house without another word. Outside, he stepped down the stairway leading to the basement, picked up his bicycle with two fingers, carried it up to the street, climbed on, and peddled briskly off to gate number 2 at the South Chicago Mills.

As soon as the door closed, the girls burst into laughter. "Poor Pa! He's so funny."

"He's a comedian and doesn't know it." Dorothy mimicked her father's frown and set Mary off again.

"He'll never learn."

"The trouble is, he won't listen. His mind is always made up. He's so stubborn. He thinks he knows everything."

Mary dipped her longjohn into her coffee. "I wish we could get him to learn how to drive a car. Then maybe we could talk him into buying one."

Dorothy shook her head ruefully. "You know that's only an excuse. He probably already knows how to drive, but won't admit it, because then he'd have no excuse for not buying one."

Mary started to say something when she was interrupted by Mama Genesyk calling from the bedroom: "Did he eat his breakfast?"

The girls sighed and exchanged glances. "Yes, Ma, he ate his breakfast."

They scurried about the kitchen then, washing the dishes, brushing crumbs off the oilcloth tablecloth that Mama had won at the Chicago Century of Progress. They made the kitchen as spotless as it had been left by Mama the night before. Then they gathered their books, put on their brown cloth jackets and scarlet babushkas, and went to the bedroom.

"Ma, you stay in bed today, okay?" Dorothy said sternly.

"I be all right," Mama answered.

"Never mind 'all right,'" Mary scolded. "You stay in bed, that's all."

"We'll be home right after school," said Dorothy. "Never mind the house. We'll clean when we get home."

"I was going to do the kitchen walls today," said Mama.

"Ma, we'll do the walls! Don't worry! Stay in bed!"

"I be all right little while."

Both girls could not escape the mute apology in their mother's eyes. It made them flee from the room. "Go way," Mama waved. "Go to school. I be all right."

As they left the house, Mama heard them. She heard their gay chatter as they passed through the gangway that separated theirs and the Sick Wife's look-alike, six-room, red brick bungalow. She listened in a mood of wonderment, almost astonishment at being alone. To lay perfectly still and hear the beat of one's own heart, the sound of one's breathing, the pulsing of blood through the veins. And radiating out from there, household sounds: the alarm clock ticking accusingly in the kitchen, the drip-drop of water from the kitchen tap, the murmurs of complaint from the oil furnace; the countless grunts and groans of the house itself, from foundation to eaves, as it withstood the wintry thrusts from outside. And from the distance, other sounds, more urgent: the high, shrill blast of a whistle that signaled the start of the morning shift at the mills for Papa and all the others. Another whistle from far off, this one so forlorn, so mournful and prolonged that it made her blood run cold—this would be an Illinois Central train on the other side of Lake Calumet. These were the worse sounds of all, sounds of a world *on it's feet*, meeting another day with courage, strength, and no complaints.

Mama Genesyk gave a little cry. She could not withstand the tidal wave of guilt any longer. She made a move to get up. Instantly, a thousand knives tore at her abdomen and she fell back in sheer agony. It was so bad that her breath was gone, which frightened her even more.

She lay there in a state of exhaustion, perspiration beginning to pour. She closed her eyes, but that only made it worse. She opened them again, stared mutely at the blue ceiling. Ah, the shame of it. She prayed for forgiveness. If this was the way it was going to be, then better to die. Yes, Papa was right. She had heard his words. Yes.

Then she closed her eyes again, as if to hide from it all. She turned her head toward the wall and groaned softly. Where could she hide from this terrible shame of being unable, for the first time in her life, to get up and face the day? Outside, the wind sang its sad lamentation and gave her terrible visions.

One gets used to anything, even pain, although in truth, the pain did subside slightly after one hour. But the relentlessly accusing sounds of the world on its feet, now magnified beyond endurance, were too much to bear. With effort, she pushed herself to a sitting position directly in front of the crucifix on the far wall, with its shredded fronds of dried yellow palm from Easter the year before.

Pushing her fist into her stomach somehow seemed to equalize the pain; enough, at least, to enable her to stagger to her feet. She leaned against the wall for support. "Jesus, Mary, and Joseph," she mumbled, "it's better. It will be all right."

Somehow she managed to slip into a gingham dress that

buttoned down the front. Slowly, she buttoned three buttons; that would be enough to make it hold. The Monday list ran through her mind. Scrub the kitchen floor, always on Monday, because of the busy weekend. Washing the kitchen walls was also on the list; they hadn't been touched since last fall. Also, the back hall. But if she could do the kitchen walls and the floor, it wouldn't be too bad.

The pain did not leave, nor did it get worse. Tears came to her eyes, however, and she blamed this on a cold that always made them watery in the mornings. Pushing her fist into her stomach again, she began scrubbing the floor. But progress was slow. By early afternoon she had finished the floor and celebrated with a cup of black coffee and a slice of black bread. Mrs. Tupacaitus, her neighbor on the other side, saw her through the window. She raised her window and yelled: "Yoo-hoo! Come over. I made fresh coffee."

Mama Genesyk did not even bother to get up. She simply waved her hand, no. She did so with some regret, however, as she had a feeling that Mrs. Tupacaitus had news about the Sick Wife. No time for gossip today. Indeed, she wasn't even sure she wanted to know how the Sick Wife was doing. The Monday list, that was all that mattered.

She emptied the dirty scrub water, cleaned the bucket, and refilled it in preparation for the walls, when suddenly she grew faint. The food she had eaten brought a rush of agony worse than any pain before. A fiery pain erupted in her lower abdomen. She pressed hard with her fist, but this time it did no good. The pain moved suddenly to her lower spine, a new area, and struck with such force that she shuddered from the convulsion of it. Dropping the wash rag on the floor, she staggered into her room and collapsed headlong onto the bed.

At five thirty-five, five minutes later than usual, Papa Genesyk arrived home. He carried a package wrapped in brown paper under his arm. His coarse, leathery features had the benign look of a contented man.

Dorothy was in the kitchen preparing supper, her mood somber with the thought of how she had come home from school and found her mother sprawled unconscious on the bed. Even with smelling salts, it had taken a long time to revive her. Mary had arrived shortly thereafter, and together they had finished the kitchen walls because Mama entreated them, almost tearfully, that if they did not do it, she would get up and do it herself.

Dorothy could not bring herself to tell Papa what had happened, especially since he seemed in such good spirits. With a silly, conspiratorial grin, he slapped the package on the table: "Where's Mary?"

"Next door, visiting the Sick Wife."

"What for? We got plenty troubles of our own. Where's my old woman?" Without waiting for the answer, he marched into the bedroom. There lay Mama, propped up on pillows, looking pale and bewildered.

"You lazy . . ." he cried cheerfully. "Whatsamatter? Still gotta bellyache?"

Mama smiled feebly. "I be all right."

"Stay in bed all day. Such a big fat lazy!" He stomped out in high humor, his spirits seeming to soar even higher at the sight of Mama. "I don't understand people today," he said. "Alla time sick. No good, I tell you." He began singing a risqué Lithuanian ballad in a guttural, off-key voice. Today had been good. The hangover had faded by ten o'clock. His thoughts, for some reason, had wandered back in time to the Old Country. To Lithuania. To Grinkiskis, his native village.

Dorothy, sniffing the odor emanating from the package, asked, "What's in the package, Pa?"

"Never mind. A secret."

"It's no secret. It stinks!"

"'Course it stinks. Stinks good! It's carp!"

"Who wants to eat that smelly thing? I'm cooking pigs' feet."

"Not for me. No pigs' feet. I cook my carp. I eat him."

"No, you don't," said Dorothy. "It'll smell up the house."

Mama's plaintive voice came from the bedroom. "I cook it for him. I know how he likes it." She knew, too, where his mind had been that day; whenever he thought about the Old Country, he brought home a carp.

Papa's grin broadened until he had the foolish look of an errant child. "Never mind," he boasted. *"Ne jus gulikite lovoje. As pats isivirsiu!,"* which meant: Stay in bed!

"Yes, Ma," Dorothy chimed. "You stay in bed."

Papa began unwrapping the evil-smelling thing. "Never mind. I cook this little doll myself."

"Where you gonna cook it, Pa?"

"Never mind. I gotta way."

"How?"

"Inna furnace."

"In the *furnace?*"

"Onna stick."

"Pa, you're goofy."

"Sure, goofy. You go to hell. I cook him."

"It's an oil burner, Pa. You'll get oil fumes all over it."

"No, no, no," said Papa, as gleeful as a boy with a new toy. "Whatsa difference what kind of fire? Fire's a fire."

With that, Papa marched triumphantly down to the basement with his prize under his arm. He spread the package on an overturned tomato crate, whittled a lathe to a sharp point, then impaled the fish. He thrust it into the oil furnace and held it near the blue flame. It seared nicely. "Aaah," he sighed. What contentment. Only one thing was lacking: a bottle of cold beer.

"Dorothy!" he roared. "Bring a beer!"

She brought it quickly, not out of fear, so much as the worry that he might come traipsing back upstairs with his smelly carp.

Papa pulled the tomato crate closer and sat down. Now he could do what he had had been planning to do all day—relive memories of the Old Country, of his boyhood, and the first time he had cooked carp over an open fire:

A mere boy lay on a hillside near the village of Grinkiskis; close by, the stream Susve. He was frightened because he was only seven and it was late at night; but he was excited, too, for he was on his own. He had run away that day and knew he would return, but not for a few days—not until he had proven to himself that he had courage. Danger lurked out there in the darkness as he dangled a freshly caught carp over a crackling fire he had built with no trouble at all.

As he roasted the fish he heard a wagon-load of Gypsies on a nearby road. The men were drunk. Their laughter and singing thrilled him. He had a sudden urge to join them. What better way to see the world! But finally their voices trailed off and all he could hear was the barking of one of their dogs.

Soon he became unaccountably lonely. He began to cry. What a silly thing to do, he chided himself. Why was he cry-

ing when his heart was so full of love for everyone? [Was it because the world was such a cruel place, filled with misery and loneliness?] He ate the carp in this mood. It was delicious! By far the tastiest dish he had ever eaten. He knew that he would never forget this night.

Then he lay back and tried counting the stars. That soon became monotonous, so he simply lay there, tremulous and moved, thinking about the immense size of the universe, the kinds of people he would meet in the world, whether he would ever get a chance to go to America. He asked himself the question: Would he ever be happier than he was at this moment? The answer was no. Yet if true, why was he so lonely, so filled with sadness? He had no answer to this question and soon fell asleep. And then . . .

But, by then, the carp was done. Maybe overdone. It had caught fire a few times in the white-hot heat, but he didn't care. The dream had been relived.

Then he noticed his beer was gone.

"Dorothy!" he hollered upstairs. "More beer!"

"No more left," Dorothy answered. "That was the last bottle."

Papa cursed, furious at this interruption in his schedule. What good was carp without beer? Mary was not yet home, and if he ordered Dorothy to go after some, she'd take too long. The only thing to do was to go for it himself—on his bicycle, quickly, to Vladek's saloon a block away—and get back before the carp got cold. If necessary, he could stick it back in the furnace to warm it up. Tenderly, he laid the fish on the brown wrapping paper, then pulled the edges around it to keep in the warmth. He rushed upstairs for his leather jacket and noticed that Dorothy was in the bedroom, serving her mother a bowl of soup.

"Where you goin', Pa?" Dorothy asked.

"Never mind."

The two women heard the door slam. Dorothy gave a rueful laugh. "Him and that stupid fish. I wonder where he got such a crazy idea."

"I wonder how it look," Mama said.

"Who cares? It's probably burnt to a crisp. I hope it gives him indigestion."

Mama smiled at the notion of Papa getting indigestion. He could eat stones if they were covered with brown gravy.

"Ma, you still got a fever," said Dorothy, feeling her mother's brow. "I think we should call a doctor."

"Never mind. No doctor." This was the third time Dorothy had suggested one.

"But you don't look good, Ma."

"I be all right."

"Did you do any work today?"

"No."

"You're lying."

"No, no. Was just starting the kitchen walls, like I told you, when I got upset in my stomach and went to bed."

"You're lying. You did the kitchen floor."

"No, no. Just putter around a little. With the mop. Only a damp mop."

"Ma, why do you drive yourself so hard? You get sick, you work twice as hard. What for? I don't understand how you think."

Mama smiled feebly.

"Times have changed, Ma. It ain't necessary to work so hard no more. Why kill yourself? This is America. Things are different here. What are you trying to prove? You doin' it for Pa? He don't appreciate it. He don't care about anything—as long as he can get drunk on weekends."

"That's not true."

"It is true. He's strong like an ox, and he has no feelings for anyone who isn't as strong as he is."

"He's a good man."

"Well . . . he don't appreciate you, Ma. That's all I'm trying to tell you. Times have changed."

Ah, yes, Mama thought. Times indeed had changed. How often had she heard that from her daughters? She was getting weary from hearing it. She had to agree with Papa that sometimes their daughters seemed to have *too many* modern ideas.

Papa came in just then, breathless from peddling his bicycle, clutching a quart of beer. He gazed at Mama from the doorway, his expression a mixture of curiosity and disdain, with even a trace of pity.

"How you feel?"

"I be all right."

"Hope so." Silence hung between them for a moment, filled with things that Dorothy would never understand. Papa said, finally: "Yeah. You be all right." Then he disappeared down the stairs to his beloved prize in the brown paper.

On the heels of this, the kitchen door opened and slammed a second time. Mary had arrived. She stripped off her jacket and babushka in the bedroom doorway—her expression grave, her lips trembling.

"Ma, please! Don't work so hard. Ma, take it easy!"

"Whatsamatter?"

Mary was crying. "The Sick Wife. She's gonna die! Tonight!"

"How you know?" asked Mama.

Dorothy interjected at the same time: "What a terrible thing to say."

"But it's true!" continued Mary. "I was there. They had the priest. He's still there. There's no hope."

Suddenlly they heard a crash. From the basement. Followed by what sounded like a firecracker going off. Then a litany of curses that made the women stiffen. Another crash. The sound of objects being thrown around. An animal's cry. The sound of shattered glass.

Papa had broken a window. He was in such a rage he sounded like he had gone crazy.

"My God!" Dorothy exclaimed. "What's going on down there?" She ran down the stairs, Mary behind her.

There, the two girls saw Papa Genesyk brandishing a poker at his mortal enemy—Greta Garbo, the family cat. Obviously, from the bones on the floor, Greta Garbo had eaten the carp.

"You sonofabitch, you die tonight!" Papa was saying to the terrified cat hiding behind the wash tubs. Papa had thrown something through the window above the tubs. His torrent of obscenities came so fast the girls only caught fragments of it: " . . . I kill you for sure, cat . . . say your prayers, cat . . . after that I throw you in the furnace, you sonofabitch . . ."

Dorothy screamed at Papa. Mary flung herself in front of the laundry tubs. Dorothy cried, "No, no, Pa! Greta's pregnant. She's gonna have babies!"

"Who care? I kill them, too. I kill every cat I see from now on."

"No, Pa! She's gonna have babies. You can't do it."

"I get 'em, I get 'em. Get outta my way . . ."

While Dorothy clung to her father, Mary managed to

reach under the tub, seize the terrified animal, and run upstairs with it. She quickly thrust the cat out the back door, where it scampered off the porch. Then Mary went downstairs to help her sister calm Papa. It took the full efforts of the two of them to make him rational again.

Later, while Papa was in the kitchen angrily devouring pigs' feet, the girls were upstairs in their mother's bedroom, reliving the scene and trying in vain to wipe the tears of laughter from their eyes. Mama was laughing heartily, too. The girls squealed and had to press their sides.

"It was unbelievable, Mama. It really was . . ."

"There was Papa with the poker . . ."

"And such an expression on his face I never saw. He would have killed the Pope, I think."

"Poor Greta. She had only one minute to live. He had the big poker and was jabbing it under the tub."

"He'd already broken a window, which only made him madder."

Mary went into another paroxysm as she remembered, "He kicked at Greta with his foot and hit the tub and almost broke his toe!"

"Poor Papa . . ."

"Lucky Greta." All this was too much for Mama. They had to give her water. Altogether it was a wonderful moment, one of those memories that families remember ever after. In this rapt mood, they recalled other memories of Papa. Papa, the stern. Papa, the fool. Papa, the clown. Papa walking through a plate glass window one Sunday in his spotless ice-cream suit. Another Sunday, Papa showing off on his bicycle, riding backward until he hit a chuckhole and fell off into a puddle of water. Did the poor ice-cream suit ever survive a weekend without having to be cleaned? they asked each other. *Never!*

The doorbell rang. Mary went to answer it. She returned a moment later, her face ashen, her expression a commingling of quiet horror and numbed disbelief.

"The Sick Wife is dead," she whispered.

"Oh my God!"

Mama began mumbling. "Jesus, Mary, and Joseph . . . spare her eternal soul . . ."

They paid their respects to the death in stunned silence.

Dorothy, some time later, asked, "When? When did she die?"

"A few minutes ago. Mrs. Tupacaitus was there. She told me."

Silence again. A few minutes ago? When they had been laughing so hard? How cruel to think that while one laughs, another dies. But that was the way life worked. The poor Sick Wife who suffered so much and so long, and never complained. The one who brought a quality of love and mercy into the neighborhood that it never had before.

"We must make some things for the wake. There will be hungry people," Mama said.

"Yes."

Papa Genesyk, oppressed by the strange silence, grew suspicious. "What's wrong?" he called from the kitchen.

Mary tiptoed out and told him. She returned, shrugging to indicate that Papa had given no reaction. "He just frowned."

A minute later Papa appeared. "It's a good thing," he tersely announced.

"Why, Pa?"

"It's not good being sick alla time. She couldn't work.

Was good for nobody. Best thing what happened. Best for everybody." The girls expressed their shock at such heartless words. Mama remained expressionless.

"Whatsamatter people today?" he went on, shaking his head. "Alla time get sick. No good." He stomped back to the kitchen, the girls following.

"Pa, what a terrible thing to say. What if it happened to you?"

"Don't care. I never get sick. Got all my teeth. My woman never gets sick. Bellyache once in a while, thatsall. People too soft today. Don't like work hard. Sick people should get better. Else die." The girls registered astonishment. Such a cruel man. How could such a man be respected, even if he was their father?

Papa, deep in his own thoughts, ignored them. Death, while no damn good, had to be respected. Recognized. He saluted it with a shot of whiskey and a glass of beer. Should go see young Stanley, the husband, he told himself. Maybe take him to Vladek's and get him drunk. No, that wouldn't work. Death meant trouble for everybody. Friends would be coming to the house. Maybe take the bottle and go over there. Pour Stanley a stiff drink and tell him to take his sorrow like a man.

All at once the three felt the presence of another person in the kitchen. They turned and saw Mama Genesyk standing there in the doorway, clad in her robe, bent over, clutching her side.

The girls gasped. "Ma, get back in bed!"

"I be all right," Mama mumbled, trying hard to smile. "I feel better."

"No, Ma. Please!"

"I feel fine."

"See?" cried Papa. "My woman don't get sick. Little bellyaches, thatsall. You look good, Sophie. You look better." He laughed at the girls, his voice a mixture of scorn and triumph. "You girls be like her, understand? Work hard. Grow strong. No complain. Be like your Mama. She show you how, hey old woman?"

Mama smiled and acknowledged with a little nod of her head. Then she hobbled over to the sink, and with great effort, began washing the supper dishes. The girls watched, open-mouthed and stricken, tears welling up in their eyes.

Later that evening, the girls sat in the dining room under the Tiffany lamp pretending to do their homework, but in truth, they were talking in muffled tones about what fate had wrought today. Papa Genesyk was next door trying to get Stanley Krystosik drunk. Mama Genesyk was back in bed, groaning softly at the pain that had returned. Her fingers were working beads in honor of the soul of the Sick Wife.

The girls, conscious of the coincidence of events of that day and too frightened to talk about its message of foreboding, spoke of other things. They talked about Russ Columbo's singing style as compared to Rudy Vallee's. They talked of President Roosevelt's latest fireside chat, because Dorothy had to write a review of it for civics class.

They talked about Keltnor, the young man who had asked Dorothy for a date several times recently.

"I don't think I like him," said Dorothy.

"Why not?"

"I don't understand him. He's such a dreamer. He talks crazy. About going off into the world and devouring it."

Mary laughed. "What does that mean?"

31

"I don't know."

"He sounds weird."

"Not weird. Just strange."

The Atwater Kent radio played softly in the background, its static almost concealing the strains of Ben Bernie's orchestra playing from New York City.

"I've made up my mind," said Dorothy later. "I'm not going out with Keltnor."

"That's up to you."

"I'd much rather have a date with Felix Szakach. He stopped by my locker again today." Felix Szakach. The all-state guard. Polish.

"Who wouldn't?" said Mary.

The Letter Writer

It's really very funny what the grape off the vine will do. For some it solves all of life's problems. For me, it solves nothing. My head goes around and I can't remember what I'm thinking. I sing. Oh, how I sing!

Oh Mama, that's the gal for me . . .
Oh Mama, that's the gal for me.

Now there is something people should do more of. Sing, I mean . . .

But I'm getting off my subject. What I started to say is, all of us were hanging around Mooney Rondo's Saloon one night, (you know where that is) when it happened. What I'm going to tell you, I mean.

We were sitting there, or standing around the way you do in saloons, talking. I can't remember about what, particularly. Anything you talk about in a saloon sounds important, ever notice that?

Well, there we were, Gabby Kowalsky and me. We got talking real important. Trying to solve the problems of life. One thing led to another. . . . We talked about insecurity, jobs, getting married, philosophy. . . . You know, what's-it-all-about?—that kind of stuff.

As I say, we were talking . . . it's funny about taverns and beer. How important they make you feel, I mean. There you are, standing a certain way, your shoulders kind of hunched forward, elbows on the bar. You feel important, like a captain giving his troops the word. You're sure everyone is looking at you, so you have another beer; you drink it casual, as through you didn't care who looked. Maybe the evening is beautiful and cool. A Sunday evening in summer, let's say. Couples passing outside, walking arm in arm so the girls can show off their fancy dresses, their figures, and who they're going with. You feel more important than them because you're alone. No skirts around your neck tonight. You're wolfing it. Those poor punks, you think. They'll have kids in a couple of years. Be tied down so tight they can't move. Then where'll they be?

That's the way I felt, talking with Gabby that night in Mooney Rondo's Saloon on the south side of Chicago. Gabby works in the shops. He runs a stamping machine. It's hard work. He doesn't always feel like going out. I don't get a chance to be with him too much. Anyhow, what can a guy like that talk about? I mean, how much does he feel like talking after running a hammer all day and pulling disks? The funny part of it is, Gabby likes to talk. He's a very serious-minded guy.

"It's funny about people," Gabby was saying.

I agreed. "Yes, people certainly are funny."

Gabby had finished telling me about a friend of his who had died, an old Polack in the mills. This Polack had saved up money all his life so he could make a trip to see the mountains in the West. This was all he talked about. Fellows would kid him about it. "Hey, Sadoski, why you wanna go West? All you gotta do is go on top the big buildings in Chicago. You can see the Rocky Mountains from there."

"Sure, Sadoski. Save lotta money. From the Wrigley Building you can see Pike's Peak so clear you think you can touch it."

Sadoski wasn't *that* dumb. He knew they were kidding him. He kept right on saving his money. He saved so much he could afford to spend six months any place he wanted. He could pick any mountain in the U.S., including Canada. So he brought his ticket, and the day he was set to go, poor Sadoski got sick and died. He never got west of Cicero. Which, to put it plain, is a rotten deal. But the point I want to bring out is, later, his friends were talking about Sadoski. Do you know that Sadoski had a feeling he wasn't *going* to make that trip? When it came time to go, he figured his life would be up. It's true. He got so nervous about it, his friends had to drag him down to the ticket office. The one thing he wanted most *not* to do was make that trip. And sure enough, as soon as he put his hands on that ticket, he died. I mean, the next morning he got sick, and in a week he was dead.

"Life really is funny," Gabby said. I nodded my head.

We were good friends, Gabby and me. Sometimes when you got a good friend to talk to, and you let conversation drift to all kinds of things, you get the feeling that you've stumbled onto some sort of big secret.

"People aren't predictable," Gabby said. "Take my brother, for instance."

"What about your brother?" I asked.

"He's a strange sort of guy. But you'd never think it to look at him."

"Of course not," I agreed. I knew Gabby's brother and he always looked okay to me. Of course, you can't always go by looks.

"Do you know what he does?" Gabby asked.

"What?"

"He writes things."

"He does?"

"Yeah."

"What kind of things?" I was more than a little puzzled.

"It's hard to explain."

"You mean like . . . stories or something?"

"Naw. Nothing like that."

"Well, like what?" Gabby paused. I could see he was having a hard time describing it. Suddenly it came to him.

"He writes letters," said Gabby. "To himself."

"To himself? What kind of letters?"

"All kinds of letters. I find 'em in his coat pockets. All kinds."

"Does he show 'em to anybody? Or send 'em to anybody?"

"Hell no!" said Gabby. "He ain't that nuts. When he gets through with 'em, he tears 'em up—unless he forgets to. But that's what I'm trying to tell you. He's screwy that way. He just writes things."

Gabby then pulled a paper folded several times over from his pocket. There was spaghetti sauce smeared on it. "Here's one I found and I forgot to tear up. I'll tear it up after you get through reading it. Don't tell him I showed it to you, okay?"

"Of course not," I said.

"This one's about a dame. And it's pretty hot stuff." Gabby laughed. "I think I know the babe he's talking about."

He handed me the paper and I began reading.

Take it from me—never go thinking one dame is better than the rest!

I wish all guys in the steel mills knew that. All guys in the world, in fact. Women are all the same, and when a guy starts getting fancy ideas about one being better than another, he better go get his head examined.

Jeez-a-man, I sure learned my lesson. Did I! It gets me so mad that every time I think of it, I could shoot myself.

The first thing, to begin with, it's my own damn fault for going to Capparelli's saloon in Hegewisch. I should stay out of that town. That town and Calumet City. I get in nothing but trouble in both them towns. I should have gone to Indiana Harbor to that new upstairs joint and got my nuts cracked like I first said I was gonna.

I'm just vain I guess. The other guys who work my shift go out with Louie so they can be seen riding with him in his new Ford convertible on Saturday nights. Like a dummy, I had to do the same thing. All we ever do is hit the joints in East Chicago, Cal-City, Indiana Harbor, and Hammond. Plus the roadhouses along the way. It's disgusting when I look back. First guy passes out gets dumped in the rumble seat. Pretty soon everybody is fried to the gills and there ain't nobody left to drive. Why Louie don't get that convert smashed up is more that I can see. Me, I would *never* have his luck!

I'm the goat. I'm just a goddamn fool. A sucker.

Falling for a dame. Jeez-a-man!

It all started when Lige came up to me one night and said, "Casper, I got a new dame I want you should meet. She's kind of screwy, I think, but she ain't having any fun."

Well, do I fall! Like ten ton of bricks. He tells me she's a distant cousin on the old lady's side (his old lady, not mine; I'm no relation to Lige). Then he give me a tune about how her folks died and she's come to town to live with Lige's folks 'cause she ain't got no place to go. The point is she don't know her way around and I got to take her under my wing.

Sucker bait, Casper, I say to myself. *You always were sucker bait.* Why should I have felt sorry for her just because she was a stranger and was scared to talk to anybody? Hell, let her get used to us. I never heard of any of us biting anybody.

That's what I say now. Why didn't I say that when I first saw her? Jeez-a-man! The first second I looked at her I could see quite distinctly she wasn't like the rest. She was sitting in a corner in Capparelli's saloon in Hegewisch, with her hands folded in her lap looking like she was scared to death. And looks! Boy, she had it over the rest of the dames in that joint. The whole town of Hegewisch in fact.

She wasn't trying to put on any airs, that much I could see. She was the straight goods. But she was scared. She had never seen a bunch of steel mill people raise hell on Saturday night. It gets pretty loud. Not that I blame the fellows. They work their ass off all week. It's their only night for fun. You know what I mean? And there's so few of us working in this goddamned Depression, plus we're all wondering who's gonna get fired next week. . . . But I can see her side, too—how easily she would get scared of all the noise and stuff.

This night, when I first met her, things were going redhot. The woman were singing and yelling their heads off. Two of them were having a fight in a corner. Some Polack was playing a mazurka on a squeezebox and everybody was slopping up beer like it was going out of style. Plus that, two broads from Cal-City were hustling the joint. Taking on guys outside on the fender of a Ford. I never had it on a fender, but they say it's fun. You can slide.

Anyhow, you can tell from this, this wasn't no joint for

a gal who was sacred. Even her lips were quivering.

I walked over to her and asked if she'd like maybe to take a walk. That was just the way I put it—with a "maybe"—so she wouldn't think I was being fresh and trying to get her outside right away for the make. I know how to act with girls like her. I think it's a crime when fellows try to get fresh and pull something on decent girls.

Well, when I asked her, she looked me straight in the eye. Right in the middle of the eye. Jeez-a-man! It was like she was looking through me. She was so pretty. Her eyes were as blue as the sky when I go to work at dawn on the early shift. Right away I realized how different she was from the rest of the dames. The rest were just dames. She was a girl. Know what I mean? Sort of a feeling goes through you. I can't describe it.

I said to myself, think of her being here with all these other bitches. I gotta get her out of here. Just seeing her in the same room with these . . . well, there's no use calling them a lot of names. You know what I mean. If you don't put your arms around 'em right away and give 'em plenty of knee-action, they think you're not a man.

Me, I'm not that kind of a guy. Oh I like mine, don't get me wrong. Who doesn't? What I mean is, a little goes a long ways with me. There's *other* things in life. I don't dream of women constantly like other guys—wet dreams all the time. You may think I'm crazy, but you know the kind of dream I like? I remember the time I dreamed I met a beautiful girl. Different from all the rest. The two of us were together. I leaned over and kissed her. Not on the lips. On the forehead. That's all I did. Nothing else. Instead of wanting more, I was satisfied. I didn't even want to touch her after that. Ain't that crazy? It just goes to show you how screwy I am.

Well, as I was saying, I went up to this girl that night and asked her if she'd like maybe to get some air. She got right up without answering and headed straight for the door. I thought it was funny at the time. Still, it was just like her. Everything she did was different.

We walked a little while, then I suggested maybe she'd like to sit in Louie's convert. (It being brand new, I figured she'd go for that.) She nodded her head yes (but didn't say a word), so we got into Louie's convert. The top was down.

We just at there. I felt funny being with her. I didn't know what to say. Usually, I can talk about anything with a dame. And if they got something I'm after, I know how to go after it.

It was nice sitting there. We could hear the music from the saloon and we could see the lights flickering in the sky from the Open Hearth in South Chicago.

Did you ever see the mills over there at night? The whole sky turns red like a cherry and lights dance up-and-down like the northern lights. It kind of scares you. She shivered a little and I told her there was nothing to be scared of. I told her about when I was a little kid and didn't know what made the sky so red. I used to shiver and think the world was coming to an end. I'd go to bed before dark and hide my head under the covers so I couldn't see those lights. But I'd lay there for hours thinking I was a coward because I was afraid to look. If I did look, I'd get terrified and would lay there all night seeing strange things on the walls of my room. I only mention this to prove what I mean when I say I am definitely screwy. I been like this all my life.

But to get back to us sitting there in the convert.

She was very close. I really felt swell. I wanted to tell her about myself. I didn't know how to go about saying it, but I wanted her to know I ain't like the rest of the Polacks and Luegins around the steel mills. I get away from them. I go out by myself. Sometimes I go to the Loop in Chicago and see the best shows. I used to always see the stage shows at the Chicago Theater, and I think it's a shame they quit. Once I even went to the Chez Paree nightclub. The tab was terrific and I couldn't afford to go back, but I tell you I felt right at home. I wanted to tell her that I'm not going to be like the rest of these foreigners I live with. I'm going to improve myself. This, to me, is a great country. Especially when we get over this fucking Depression. And if we don't, then there's no hope for any of us.

Well, anyway, that's the kind of thing I wanted to say to her. But I didn't really say a thing. The words wouldn't come. We just sat there listening to the music. It gives you a sad kind of feeling, hearing the music in the night air. Even if it's a goofy song and nothing but drunks singing it . . .

Sweet violets
sweeter than all the roses
covered all over from head to foot
covered all over with snow

That was the song they were singing inside the saloon. (Only they didn't sing it with the word "snow".)

There we sat, neither one speaking. I got puzzled. I didn't know if there was something wrong with me, or if she was waiting for me to start something, or what. That's when I did it!

Jeez-a-man! I don't know what came over me. But first thing I knew I had my hand around her waist. Then it went higher. And higher, until I had it on her you-know-what. It makes me sick to think I did that to such a sweet girl.

As soon as I did it, I wished I hadn't. But my hands were already up there, so what could I do? I was sure she'd make me take them down. But she didn't. She just wiggled a little. Sort of shivered like she was cold, that's all.

For about an hour we sat that way. The longer we sat the more scared I was to move my hands the least bit. (They felt so warm and nice.) I could feel her heart beating. It beat fast like a trip-hammer. Like if I took my hand away, her heart would stop beating altogether. What a girl!

It was funny how we didn't talk. Seemed like we didn't have to talk. I started to say a couple of words once or twice and all she'd answer is yes or no. We just sat there, and believe it or not, I felt as through I'd known her all my life.

I felt like the time I was at Flint Lake in Indiana. That's a nice, quiet summer resort. We had been there all day. A bunch of us fellows swimming and dancing in the evening. When the dance closed, the fellows went to town for some beer. I stayed behind. I don't know what came over me, but one of my crazy streaks hit me and I felt like sitting on the pier. At the edge of the water.

It was late, I remember. Fact is, it must have been about the middle of the night. I could hear oarlocks on the water. And two couples in a boat. Rowing across the lake to where their cottage was. How their voices carried. You could hear their laughter all around the lake. One of the girls laughed and said, "Jack, don't rock the boat." And of course, he rocked it some more.

Well, there I sat, so close to the water I could put my hand in it, listening to those people out there in the middle of Flint Lake. I felt sad. Sad all over. It's hard to explain. Their voices grew more faint. But I could still hear the squeaking sound of those oarlocks. Then they began singing. Laughing and singing "The Volga Boat Song."

Row boys row
row boys row

They kept it up all the way across. The last thing I heard they must have reached the other side. One of the girls laughed. Her high voice carried very clearly.

Do you know what I did? I started to cry. Yes. I cried for a long time without knowing what I was crying about. I still don't know what I was crying about.

I only mention this to explain how this was the way I felt sitting there with her in Louie's convert.

We sat there for maybe an hour. Then she said, "It's getting late. I gotta go."

"Sure," I said. But she didn't make any move to get out of the car. I figured maybe she was waiting for me to kiss her good night. To tell the truth, I didn't have the nerve. I felt like such a heel for putting my hands in such a place on her, I didn't have the nerve to kiss her. I guess I figured I done enough to her already.

Pretty soon she spoke again. "It's getting late," she said. "I got to go."

"Okay," I said. "Stay where you are. I'll get around and open the door for you." But before I could get there, she got out.

I took her back inside to Lige, my pal, and said good night. I made no mention about seeing her again. But I knew I would.

By this time, Louie and the rest were plenty drunk. They were in the mood to fight anybody in the joint. I got 'em all outside quick so she couldn't see the kind of bums I run around with.

We drove home on both sides of the road. As usual. Louie nearly passed out at the wheel, so we dumped him in the rumble seat and I drove. All the way home I kept thinking, why did I put my hands where I did? Why is it, a guy does the opposite of what he really wants? In this case, was it from force of habit? From doing it with so many other dames? I don't know. Another thing I asked myself: why didn't I kiss her good night? That was something I did want to do. Yet I didn't have the courage. Or something. Why is that?

Well, like I said, I knew it wouldn't be the last time I would see her. So a couple nights later, I borrowed Louie's convert. I took her out.

We drove around the north side of Lake Calumet, which is getting to be a big shipping port. We parked on one of the new roads they got there. The stink from Sherwin-Williams was blowing the other way, so there was no odor. Sometimes that odor from all them chemicals is enough to make you think that a chemical war has started.

Anyhow, we parked right at the water's edge. Not that Lake Calumet is much of a lake. You can walk all the way across it, if you skip the dredged channel for the big ships. It's a terrible lake, if you want to know the truth. All the factories along the shore dump their stuff into it. Catch a catfish in that lake, eat it, I swear you'll die of poisoning.

We watched the flames in the sky again and didn't do much talking. I was actually surprised when she spoke and asked me a question.

"You come by my house last night?" she asked.

I said that yes, I did. I told her I dropped by to see Lige, only the truth was, I came to see her.

She said, "Lige says you asked him where did I go?"

"That's right," I admitted. "I said, 'Lige, is your cousin

around?' He said, 'No, she went out.'"

The truth was, I knew where she went 'cause Lige had told me. But I wanted to see if she would tell me the truth by herself. Without being asked.

"Reno come by my house," she said.

"Yeah?" I said pretending I wasn't interested.

"He asked me to go out with him."

"He did? That's fine." Jeez-a-man! I thought. She's telling me the truth without being asked. She wants me to know why she wasn't home.

"I didn't know you was coming," she said.

"That's all right," I said. "I ain't got no hold on you."

"I wouldn't gone out with Reno if I known you was coming."

I felt mighty good, I tell you. "Think nothing of it," I said. But the truth was, I could've jumped out of that car and hopped a six-foot fence. At the same time, I felt sore at Reno. What did Reno want fooling around with her? I'll bust his Dago head open, I said to myself.

I was just then going to say something when she moved closer. Real close. Jeez-a-man! Did you ever have a girl sit so close you could feel how warm she is? Sort of makes you feel like she's a part of you or something?

Well, I may as well admit it. That's when the worst started.

Before I knew it I was putting my hand right back up there where it had been before. But I no sooner got it half way up when she stopped me.

"Don't," she said.

She was right. I knew. I didn't have any objections. Yet, just the same I had to know why she objected. Just because I wanted to put my hand there didn't mean I put her in the same class with all the other dames I know.

"Why can't I?" I asked.

"I don't know," she said.

This got me curious. We were different, I figured. She shouldn't put me in the same class with other guys. This wasn't one of those things like I was after it, and she was waiting to give it.

"What's the matter?" I asked.

"Nothing," she said. but she sounded all mixed up and funny-like.

"I did it last time," I said.

"I know it."

"Why can't I do it now?"

She didn't answer. So after a little while I tried again.

She stopped me again.

"What's the matter?" I said. I couldn't understand this at all.

She didn't say a word. She just moved closer till we were so tight together you couldn't have put a sheet of paper between us.

"I never went out with a man before," she said.

"What's that got to do with me?" I asked her.

"I don't know," she said.

"I don't care if you never went out with a man before," I said. "In fact, that's good. I'm just saying it feels good."

"Does it?"

"It gives me a wonderful feeling when you let me do that."

She turned and looked right into my eyes. Hard-like. "Does it?" she asked.

"It sure does."

"What kind of feeling?"

"I don't know. It's just . . . wonderful!" Jeez-a-man! How could I tell her what kind of feeling? Well this got her excited. She held on to me like we were on a boat that was rocking. I never saw a girl act that way before. She looked at me, waiting for me to say something. But I was afraid that whatever I'd say would be the wrong thing. So I kept my mouth shut, which is always a smart thing for me to do.

"All right," she said all of a sudden. "You can do it."

"I can?"

She took my hand and with her very own hand put my hand . . . not *up* where it had been before, but *down . . . way down . . . you-know-where!* Jeez-a-man! I tell you this was incredible. I didn't believe what was happening.

I didn't believe she was that kind! It shows you how you can get fooled. After all, putting my hand up . . . high, where it had been the night before, that, I figured was all right. . . . But this . . . on the second night we were together . . . I was shocked.

She saw how surprised I was, but I guess she mistook my feelings and thought I was pleased. "It's allright," she said. "You can do it."

What was I supposed to say? What would you say? I couldn't say a thing.

"It's all right," she said. "You can do it if it gives you wonderful feelings."

Christ Almighty! What was I supposed to say? All right, baby, let's go? Only thing I remember is wanting to jump out of the car and leave her sitting there. Man was I a chump! A pushover the second night, when I was even afraid to touch her the first night. Looking back I can see it clearly. I should have taken advantage of that opportunity. But I didn't. You know what they say, another slice off a cut loaf never hurt anybody.

Anyhow, that's what happened. I never saw her again after that. But I still can't get her out of my mind. It just goes to show you what a sucker a guy can be when he lets himself get fancy ideas about women.

I'm a fall guy and always will be. Any dame can come along I guess and take me for a ride. I never did go much for that bull about love and all but Jeez-a-man, if only a guy could find the right girl. A guy can't go roaming around by himself all the time. He's got to have somebody who understands.

I keep wondering how it would have turned out if she hadn't . . . you know what. Was she a real virgin? Was she really giving herself to me because she felt like I did and didn't know any better? Or had that Reno broke her in? We would have been married by now. 'Cause I would have asked her for sure. We'd've got a little apartment in Hammond or Cal-City. They got 'em cheap over there. We could've got started out in life.

I could kill that dirty bastard Reno. I bet it's all his fault. That look in her eyes . . . I can still see it. She probably don't even know such a thing is bad. . . . She's so inexperienced I bet it never occurred to her that you gotta save it.

Somehow I can't get her off my mind. If only that night hadn't happened that way, there'd be more to my life than working for a goddamn steel mill and whoring around all night with a bunch of goddamn bums.

Tonight I feel like getting drunk. Only I did that last night . . .

Maybe if I got to Capparelli's again, I'll see her. I could see Lige at least. Maybe he could tell me where she is . . .

Jesus, I'm lonely . . .

The letter ended there.

I folded the paper and gave it back to Gabby. He folded it up and put it in his pocket.

"See what I mean?" he said.

"Yes, I see." The same feeling came over me as before. I was certain of only one thing: I sure discovered something about Casper. I had always thought him to be such a quiet guy. Hardly ever said anything.

"Look," said Gabby. "Don't hold it against him."

"Hold *what* against him?"

"Writing them crazy letters like this."

"Why should I?" I said to Gabby. "I always liked Casper."

"I know. . . . What I mean is, if anybody else knew he wrote letters to himself, they'd think he was off his rocker. You know how guys are around here."

"I know."

"Keep it to yourself. He'll get over it. Don't hold it against him, will you?"

"Of course not, Gabby," I said.

"'Cause otherwise he's a hell of a guy."

"Sure he is," I agreed.

We ordered two more beers and began talking about the White Sox. Then Keltnor walked in. Jeez, we hadn't seen him for over a year. Last time I knew, he was bumming around the country. Gosh, it was good seeing Keltnor again. He looked great. Said he was only going to hang around for a few days, then hit the road again. He was very tan, thin, and, you know, tight in the face. Like he was living with everything he had.

We told Keltnor about Casper, the Letter Writer, because Casper and Keltnor had always been good friends.

No, that is not quite correct. We didn't mention the letter-writing part at first, because that was supposed to be a secret between Gabby Kowalsky and me. We just said we'd been talking about Casper. Well, Keltnor wanted to know all about how Casper was, and so forth. But then we had a few more beers and we told Keltnor about Casper's crazy habit of writing letters to himself. Gabby showed Keltnor the letter Casper had written.

Let me tell you, Keltnor got red in the face and blew up right there. He told us to quit stomping on Casper's soul—whatever the hell that meant. If you know Keltnor, you know that sometimes he can be a little vague.

Keltnor tore the letter into tiny pieces. He went into the can and flushed it down the toilet. When he came out, he said, "Now maybe you guys will leave Casper alone."

Leave him alone? What did we do?" I asked. " I like Casper. I got nothing against Casper."

"Sure," said Gabby. "He's my brother. Would I do anything to hurt my own brother?"

"You're both full of shit," said Keltnor and he walked away. A week later, he left town again. I haven't seen him since.

I don't know how it happened, or who started it—except it wasn't me—but, from that day on, poor Casper got the name of the Letter Writer. He is still called that to this day. At first he used to get upset about it. But now he doesn't seem to mind.

What the hell. You can get used to anything, I always say.

The Family Dombrowski

The Devil seldom announced himself when he came to the house of Leo Dombrowski. Slyly he would slip by the holy water fount inside the door of the red brick bungalow, and simply set up camp. One never knew how long he would stay, but his presence was usually felt. Maryusha Dombrowski, the mother, had a sixth sense about it. On such occasions, she would dip into the seraph-encrusted porcelain fount and liberally sprinkle the precious drops in every direction. Not that the water was to be wasted: A full pint fetched one dollar and fifty cents at St. Casimir's Polish Roman Catholic Church.

Today the Devil was certainly there. He had most of the household in his grip, and was running amuck amongst the spirits of the two sons: John, nineteen, and Joseph, eighteen. Maryusha Dombrowski went to the fount three times that morning. By noon it was empty. Leo Dombrowski, of course, knew nothing about this, because he was at work at the Drop Forge plant; not did Frank, the eldest son, because he, too, was a man, and had a job at the Novack Accounting Company.

But fourteen-year-old Sophia Dombrowski knew. And she found the excitement unbearably pleasurable. A day like this had not come around for as long as she could remember. She could scarcely wait to tell her eleven-year-old brother, Aloise, when he came home from school for lunch. Today was one of those days when Sophia did not regret being unable to attend high school; although, on other days, she resented it very much. The Dombrowski parents believed that high school, with its modern, corrupt ways, was no decent place for a Polish virgin of fourteen. Her place was in the home, where she could be of service and learn how to be a good housekeeper. For when she married, what other role would there be except that of mother and homemaker?

When Aloise got home at ten minutes after twelve, he knew something was wrong even before Sophia could tell him.

"Hey, there's no holy water. What's wrong?"

"Shh! Come with me. I'll tell you." Sophia took him into the bathroom and closed the door. "Oh, Aloise, it was too much to believe. You should have seen them."

"Seen who? Don't talk so fast."

"They were so brave. Both of them."

"Who? What?"

"John and Joseph."

Aloise's ears, which were too large for his stocky little body, twitched with excitement. "What did they do?"

Sophia began gesticulating wildly. "It's terrible what they did. I agreed with Mama. But, I also agree with them. After all, they're not children anymore."

"Tell me what they did."

"They walked away from Mama!"

Aloise frowned, as his father often did. He was completely baffled. John and Joseph, true, were almost grown men. Big and strong. They never walked away from a street fight; yet they never started one. But *walking away from Mama* . . . What could have gotten into them?

"They just walked away, I tell you . . . and when Mama

said, 'Yunick, I'm telling you for the last time, come back in the house,' what do you think Yunick did?"

"He came back in."

"No. They walked away. Like I said."

"Really?"

"Yes. Just like that. Both of them. And do you know what else Yunick did?"

"What?"

"He *smiled.*"

"Smiled?"

"Just like this. Like he was saying, 'I am sorry, Mama, but I'm a grown man now and I can do what I want.'"

"I don't believe it."

"True. It happened. I saw it with my own eyes. Here's how it happened . . ."

The morning had begun uneventfully enough. Leo Dombrowski had gone off to the Drop Forge at his regular time of six o'clock. A taciturn man, not given to excessive displays, Leo managed to conceal the quiet pride he felt about his status in life. Four fine sons and only one daughter—a proper combination; a red brick bungalow in the middle of a block that was marred by only two families that were not Polish: Yuktonis and Kucinskus—both, unfortunately, Lithuanians. But one could not hope for everything in life, not in these Depression times. Yet it did seem a strange act of fate, and a bit unfair, to emigrate all the way from Krakow only to find oneself living near undesirables. Not that there weren't good Lithuanians. He knew a few, but the Yuktonis and Kucinskus tribes were not among them. They were a bit loud and boastful, and in Leo Dombrowski's book, one judged a man by what he did *not* say, rather than by what he *said*.

John and Joseph Dombrowski went nowhere that morning, simply because they had no place to go. They had recently quit the manual-training high school and were waiting to be called for employment at Acme Steel. Jobs were not easy to find in 1934, in the West Pullman district of Chicago, but their uncle had "pull" at Acme and had persuaded Leo Dombrowski that it would be a waste of time for the boys to finish high school when he could get them started in the steel mill. "Better to begin seniority in something that pays wages than to fritter away one's time in school," said Uncle Sadoski.

Time, therefore, was beginning to hang heavy on the boys' hands. They were starting to grow restless. Leo and Maryusha stayed awake at night trying to figure out chores to keep them busy. They had painted the basement; manured the lawn; cemented cracks in the front steps; cleaned out the garage, attic, and basement; and now there was nothing left for them to do.

But today they were to be on hand starting at eight o'clock to supervise the dumping of two tons of coal at the curb. And at nine o'clock, or whenever the coal had been dumped, they were to begin hauling it to the basement by wheelbarrow.

By eight-fifteen, the coal had been dumped. Calumet Coal & Coke was always prompt in its deliveries, despite the fact that their coal was too soft and dirty. For the next forty-five minutes, after the coal had been dumped, the brothers stood at the curb, looking at it.

Mama Dombrowski said nothing. She knew the boys were testing her. After all, Papa had said, "Start hauling it in *no later* than nine o'clock." Dumping coal on the street was a dirty business. It was a matter of pride to get the mess cleaned up as soon as possible. So the boys, Mama Dombrowski knew, were purposely waiting until the very last minute.

At two minutes before nine, Joseph remembered something he had forgotten to do. He had promised to inspect a friend's rabbit hutch a block away.

Mama Dombrowski, watching from behind the lace curtains in the living room, saw the boys begin to walk down the street.

"Yunick. Yusiff. Where you going?"

"Down the street," Joseph replied.

"It's nine o'clock. Do the coal."

"We'll be right back. We'll only be a few minutes."

"Do the coal," Mama said.

"We'll be right back."

"Do it now."

And so, the battle was joined. The two brothers stood there, looking at each other and at the coal, but not at Mama. Then Mama's voice began to rise. In Polish. Heads began to peer out of windows. Notably, those of Mrs. Yuktonis and Mrs. Kucinskus. As Sophia described it, this had to be "most humiliating" for the boys. After all, they were not children any longer. John was six feet, two inches tall, and very muscular. He weighed 210 pounds. Joseph was an inch taller; but slender and lighter.

"We'll be back in five minutes," said John in the same patient voice his father used.

"No! Do what I say!" Mama was in something like a rage by now. She commanded the two of them to return to the house at once.

"This," said Sophia, "is when I saw Yunick smile."

Aloise was fascinated. "Smile?" He had never heard anything like this.

"Yes. *Smile.* I saw this with my own eyes."

Aloise rubbed his chin like his father often did. "Well, if you saw it, I guess it must have happened. But, what happened to the coal? It's not there."

"Of course, it's not there. They came back in an hour and hauled it in. That's not the point. The point is they *disobeyed* Mama. Right to her face. In public! Where everyone could see, including those two old hens, Yuktonis and Kucinskus."

Aloise had to agree with that. To openly disobey one's own mother was bad enough, but to do it in front of others! Well! Tonight, for sure, was going to be a special occasion. When Mama told Papa about it . . . oh, what a beating there would be from Papa! Aloise began thinking of places he could hide without missing the action. *No wonder the holy water was gone!*

"Where are Yunick and Yusiff now?" he asked, thinking at the same time, *I've got to find them!*

"Who knows?" said Sophia. "They disappeared."

"Disappeared? You think they ran away?"

"Who knows? They went down the alley and that's the last I saw them."

Aloise began fidgeting. The excitement had spread all the way down to his kidneys. He asked Sophia to leave so he could take care of the problem. While the water was flushing, he shuddered with the delicious excitement of it all. Sophia was right. Nothing like this had ever happened before. This, indeed, was a day to be around, while somehow making himself scarce. A day to keep one's eyes and ears open, to miss nothing. Meanwhile, he told himself, he *must* find Yunick and Yusiff.

After hauling in the coal, the Dombrowski brothers took a walk to collect their thoughts. Then they returned to the alley behind their house, where they propped themselves up against a wooden fence and began reading comic books they had culled from a neighbor's garbage can.

For a long while they did not talk. They were so close, words were not necessary between them. John, the older, was introverted. He kept to himself much of the time; he would shoot free throws by the hour at the rim of an old tomato basket that hung from the garage door, or practice place-kicking in a lot nearby. Success at anything came slowly for John, but he practiced with such fierce determination that he usually managed to master whatever he was trying to do. On one Fourth of July, he practiced pool shots in the basement on the table Leo Dombrowski had purchased secondhand so that his boys could play pool at home, and not in pool rooms. On this occasion, John practiced for twelve hours, eventually improving his game enough to beat his ubiquitous Irish rival, Tommy Touhy. Now, he concentrated intently on the captions of *Captain Marvel*, using his finger to point out the difficult words.

Joseph, on the other hand, was one to whom things came easily. He was better coordinated than his older brother and could beat him at most games, unless John decided to make a special project of the matter, as he did with place-kicking and pool. Joseph also had a short temper, which his older brother often warned him about. For that reason, Joseph went to great lengths to avoid fights, because when the veins in his temple began to twitch, his fists would lash out; after that, there was no stopping him. He hung on to his opponent like a bulldog and had to be pulled off.

On the other hand, Joseph had another problem which his older brother did not: He was terrified of girls. Not sexually. He enjoyed his experiences with the whores in Gary, Indiana Harbor, and East Chicago—whenever he could earn the dollar-and-a-half that such pleasures cost. But with decent girls he was something of a failure. He could not communicate with them. He could not bear the thought that a decent girl would do *that* with him. Therefore, he was considered something of an "oddball" by some of his friends, and certainly by the local virgins who, to be sure, wouldn't go that far. But they were human, and were not averse to some respectable necking.

After laboriously following every word of the captions in *Captain Marvel* and *Flash Gordon*, John put his magazine down. He couldn't concentrate. Not that comics weren't enjoyable. But he couldn't get his mind off what he had done. What had he gotten his brother into? Such a mess. And, to make his conscience hurt worse, Joseph had *followed* him unquestioningly! Not wavered a bit. What more could one ask of a kid brother? This, he decided, he must never forget. Not if he lived to be one hundred. But why, he asked himself. Why had Joseph followed him?

"Yusiff," he asked quietly, "why did you do that?"

"Do what?"

"Follow me."

Joseph pondered the question, his expression belying his befuddlement. Unable to come up with the proper answer, Joseph shrugged. "I don't know."

"You didn't have to come."

"I know it."

"So, why did you come?"

"I don't know."

John thought, fair enough. He is certainly honest, among many other things.

"I went because you went," said Joseph finally.

"Because I went?"

"Yes."

"You feel like I do?"

"Yes."

"Why?"

"I don't know."

"If you feel that way, you must have a reason."

"I don't know," said Joseph. "I just felt that way."

"You sure?"

"Sure I'm sure."

"Okay," said John. Okay indeed. He picked up *Captain Marvel* again. What more could one ask from one's brother? He suddenly was embarrassed by the closeness he felt for him. What else was there to say? Or do? "Finished with your comics?" he asked.

Joseph said, yes, and they exchanged. *Captain Marvel* and *Flash Gordon* for *Buck Rogers* and *Tarzan*. After twenty minutes, Joseph pulled a chamois-skin pouch from his pocket. The Ingersoll watch, gleaming within, read 12:15.

"I'm so hungry," said John. "I could eat a skunk."

Joseph laughed. There was no skunk to be found, and certainly there would be no lunch today, unless they looked in garbage cans. "Just say to yourself that you're not hungry, and you won't be hungry."

"Sure," said John. They began reading again. Later, John said, half aloud, "Why did she do it?" Meaning Mama. Mama shrieking at them in front of the whole world, insisting that they come in "this minute." Didn't Mama know that they were not boys any longer, but grown men who must be treated like men? After all, they had hauled the coal in an hour later, so why all the fuss? Why embarrass them that way? Pondering that question, as he stared at a nearby garbage can he mumbled, "I don't know."

"Don't know what?" asked Joseph.

"Never mind."

"I got an idea," said Joseph. "Let's go see Frank."

"What for? What good can Frank do? He's got problems of his own."

"I know. But let's go see him."

John shrugged. "Okay. Maybe he'll loan us some money so we can eat."

Although it was only mid-morning in Novotny's Sokol Lounge, Frank Dombrowski, sitting alone at the bar, had already succeeded in getting himself partially drunk.

His friends knew why he was there. They knew he was trying to "figure things out." Trying to get to the bottom of things. The Dombrowskis were the kind to whom things did not come easily. They were not quick-witted. They had to put more effort that others did into finding solutions to problems. Yet they were tenacious.

Frank's problem was that not long ago, tragedy had struck his life. A terrible, bewildering, numbing tragedy. A tragedy of such proportion that he knew he could not go on about the business of living until he found some answers. *Some* kind of answers.

He sat in deep preoccupation at the mahogany bar, walled in by silence. Thinking for a few moments, then letting his mind go blank. Always, in between, asking the question, *why?* And tugging at all the "ifs": What if he hadn't done the foolish thing of tossing the coin? What if Maryk Nowicki, the bouncer, hadn't gotten drunk at his cousin's wedding? Yes, the "ifs" went all the way back to Maryk's cousin's wedding. How mysteriously Fate, or God, or whatever one chose to call it, worked its awful deeds.

Steve Novotny, the owner, watched his friend solicitously as Frank fingered the empty shot glass and stared into his beer. Such a handsome fellow, Steven thought, to whom sorrow like this should not have to come: square-jawed; well built; coarse, straw-blond hair; a fierce scowl; and jet-black eyes glistening with tension and questions. Steve pushed a pepper shaker forward: "Zamyslony, put a little pepper in it." As all good Poles knew, a little pepper helped to keep one from getting sick if one was determined to get drunk.

Frank's mind came back to reality. He looked startled, then pushed his empty shot glass forward. "Another boilermaker."

Steve shrugged, sighed, and walked away. Boilermakers all day long, every day—the way Frank was taking them—could scramble one's brains. But he came back with another two-ounce shot of Corbey's whiskey and another stein of beer.

Frank Dombrowski was called Zamyslony—the thinking one—because he was one of the most respected young men in the district. Not only had he graduated from high school with honors, but he had combined athletics with it. He had won the Golden Gloves light-heavy division in boxing, and had been all-city center in football for two consecutive years.

When he graduated from high school, he had a choice of *two* football scholarships; one from a Big Ten school, in itself quite an honor. Frank Dombrowski, they said, had "everything."

But, to everyone's surprise, he refused them both. The Depression did not really take hold until 1930; but even before that, layoffs at the Drop Forge Plant were frequent. Mortgage payments on the Dombrowski house had to be met, and Frank recognized his family obligation to help out. He worked days at whatever he could find, mostly hard labor. He studied accounting at night, at DePaul University. It took him an hour each night to get there by street car, and another hour to return, past midnight. With interruptions, because of occasional night jobs that paid so much they could not be turned down, it took six years for Frank to obtain his accounting degree.

In 1932 he put on a white shirt as a proud symbol of his new status, and went to work at Novack's Accounting Company for twenty-five dollars per week.

Of course, if the truth be known, there was another reason why Frank did not accept either athletic scholarship, both at out-of-town schools. That reason was Valerie Kusznitki, to whom he became engaged the year he became an accountant. She had been Frank's sweetheart since early high school. She was Polish, and beautiful. She had dark eyes, and an impetuous, mischievous manner. She liked to put creepy, crawly things into his locker, like garter snakes, toad, and snails. She was impudent. She laughed at life, not merely because she loved it so much, but because she found life actually quite funny.

And Frank idolized her. They were opposites in spirit and temperament, and this, they knew, was good for each other. From the beginning, everyone said that theirs was truly a match made in Heaven. Throughout their long courtship they took Communion daily at St. Casimir's Polish Roman Catholic Church. They were the center of attraction at picnics, bowling matches, weddings, dances, and funerals. Frank, being Zamyslony, was asked his opinion on every subject except sex. He refused to discourse on that subject. "What goes on between two people should be kept to themselves," he was fond of saying.

As the courtship progressed, the two families, who lived only a block apart, became so friendly that they began calling each other by such familiar terms as Uncle and Cousin long before their betrothal was announced.

And then it occurred.

Like most occasions of dire consequence, this one began in complete innocence. Frank tortured himself about it many days and nights afterward. How does one know when something awful is about to happen? Why can't there be some warning?

It was Saturday night in early summer, which, in Chicago, feels like late spring, because there is no true spring. Saturday night in Casper Grigunis's Balkan Tap, with the huge new Wurlitzer jukebox. The Balkan was a good saloon by any standard. But on Saturday night, merriment became intense, so much so that Casper had to have a bouncer. Maryk Nowicki was a good bouncer. He was a friendly, broken-nosed, cauliflower-eared, slightly punchy ex-boxer. On that particular day, his cousin had been married. Maryk got too happy at the wedding; when he showed up early in the evening, he staggered to the men's room, locked the door, and promptly fell asleep. Frank, never one to turn down a friend in need, offered to substitute as bouncer that night.

Valerie nursed her beers and watched proudly as Frank

kept everyone under control. The squad car that cruised the neighborhood on Saturday nights had nothing to do for the first time in months. Not a single argument had to be settled in the alley. Not that there weren't squabbles at the bar. That was to be expected. But Frank settled each and every one diplomatically, and as peacemaker, had to accept numerous drinks as a token of respect to both parties.

When the evening ended at about two in the morning, he was in a euphoric state. He announced to his fiancée that they were going to take a ride. To cool off. He put his betrothed in his six-year-old Plymouth and they began a long, meandering drive through the Calumet region: through Indiana Harbor, East Chicago, Hammond, and Gary. Then they took the Indiana toll road as far as South Bend, and doubling back through side roads, found themselves in Crown Point.

Frank stopped at the courthouse. "Know where we are?" he asked.

"Sure," said Valerie. "Crown Point."

"Know what Crown Point is famous for?"

Valerie laughed. She knew indeed. "Elopements."

Frank chuckled. "What are we waiting for?"

Valerie squealed with delight. "Frank, you're crazy."

"It's time we both got crazy. We've been engaged three years."

Her answer quite astonished him: "Okay."

The words sobered Frank up. He became rapt in thought. Then he pulled a coin from his pocket. "So you'll never blame me, we'll let the coin decide. Heads, we get married; tails, we don't."

"Okay."

Frank flipped the coin; slapped it on his wrist.

It showed heads.

Valerie cried out.

"We get married," Frank said softly, and in some amazement. Now he was unnerved by what he had done. Such foolishness, he thought; letting a coin decide such an important event. Not that their marriage wasn't inevitable. Of course it was. But to let a coin decide . . .

"A justice of the peace," Valerie said wonderingly, looking up at the courthouse. She, too, was so caught up in the ludicrousness of the situation. Two Polish Catholics married by a J.P.! What would their families think? They talked about this, and agreed within a few minutes that this was not the way.

"Okay!" said Frank irritably, as through he was the one who was giving in. "All right. All right. But we'll not wait any longer. That's for sure. Tomorrow night, understand? At your house."

"What at my house?"

"We'll tell them. Before both families. You announce the date. I don't care when it is, as long as it's no longer than two months away."

They kissed and Valerie rubbed his leg as though they were married already. They necked fiercely until a squad car cruised by and flashed its spotlight.

While Valerie straightened out her clothes, Frank started the car. Always a cautious driver, he forgot himself this one time. He failed to look back and notice the parked car that had not been there before. Valerie, with her legs curled under her, was reaching in her purse for her compact when the car surged backward and struck the other car. Her head hit the center frame post. She was stunned momentarily, although Frank scarcely noticed because he had jumped out to inspect the damage. Fortunately, there was none, other than a broken taillight on his car. He jumped back in and slammed the door.

"You all right?" he asked.

"Fine," said Valerie. She felt a slight ache at the base of her skull, but this was small price to pay for the deliciousness of the moment: to know that Frank had *purposely* driven her here to *force* her into deciding a date for their marriage!

"Two months!" Frank repeated almost savagely as he roared off. "At the most! I don't mean two months and a day. In fact, I would prefer two *weeks* and a day. But suit yourself—you pick the date, as long as it's no more than two months."

Other than a feeling of stiffness and a bruised elbow, Valerie felt fine the next morning when the two attended Mass. In the afternoon, a slight dizziness came over her, and a mild headache developed. She told Frank nothing about it. Who could complain after such an important development? The date was secretly tucked away in her mind. One month! Frank would be pleased when he heard *that*.

After Mass, the word was put out to both families. There would be an important announcement involving the Dombrowski and Kusznitki families that night. Gather at five o'clock.

In the afternoon, about four, Valerie's headache grew worse. It was not quite like any she had had before. She took three aspirin and lay down to take a nap.

She fell asleep, and when she awakened she could already hear the animated buzz from the kitchen where the families were gathered. She heard the rich, fluent cadences of Polish, the tinkling of glasses, and much laughter.

Frank came in. "Hey, sleepyhead, get up. Everyone's waiting for the announcement. I told them I know nothing about it."

"I've changed my mind," she teased. "I've decided I don't want to get married."

"Great! Now I'm off the hook. I called your bluff." His eyes rolled in mock self-pity. "A fine thing. The groom's fate is sealed and he doesn't even know the date."

"None of your business. You'll hear when the rest hear."

He left her, warning that she had only a few minutes to put her makeup on and get out there where the excitement was mounting. Returning to the kitchen, he found the boilermakers flowing well. The women were sedately sipping their beers, but were more excited than the men. Papa Kusznitki was heatedly arguing with his brother-in-law, Henry Szafranowski, about the merits of cash payments versus installment buying.

"The world has gone crazy," Papa Kusznitki was saying. "Today you pay ten dollars down and the rest when they catch you. Only the Irish do that."

"And the Armenians," said someone.

"No, not the Armenians. They believe in cash."

"Certainly not the Czechs."

"Oh, God no. They sew their money in a mattress, and then they forget which mattress and throw the wrong one out."

"Also, it makes the mattress lumpy so they don't get a good night's sleep."

This brought a roar of laughter. Certainly, no race was more cautious about their money than the Czechs, unless it was the Dutch, who were numerous in the district.

Frank surprised everyone by defending the practice of credit buying. "It's the coming thing," he said, "whether you like it or not. Some day, we'll all be doing it—Depression or not."

The families virtually laughed Frank out of the kitchen and told him to go get his girl because they were getting mighty impatient for the "announcement."

He returned a moment later with his girl. Valerie looked wan, but nevertheless radiant.

"Here's my beautiful invalid," he said. "She can make big announcements, but she can't take a little bump on her head." He swept her off her feet and deposited her in a chair, before which one of the men instantly produced a beer.

Valerie raised her glass, took one sip and then, suddenly, a look of astonishment swept over her lovely features. It was an expression of utter incredulity. She gasped, just once. Her mouth then closed quickly and she collapsed in Frank's arms.

The doctor, who came later, said it was his belief that her death had been caused by a cerebral aneurism, and that it had probably been induced by the car accident the night before.

This opinion was also shared by the doctors at the hospital where the death was confirmed.

For the next terrible days Frank remained astonishingly poised. He insisted on handling every detail of the funeral. He selected the coffin, arranged for the High Mass, saw that the proper obituary notices were placed in the papers, and even selected the cemetery plot. "She was mine," he said without emotion. "Mine, just as much as if we had been married. I will take care of everything." Tongues wagged when it was learned that he had ordered a tombstone with both names to be chiseled on it. When the salesman reminded him that this was quite unorthodox, he grabbed the salesman by the throat and began choking him.

After the funeral, Frank returned to his job seemingly with no ill effects. He resumed his regular life. He bowled with his team; assisted the coach of the Knights of Columbus basketball team in getting the team ready for the season. He played pool occasionally at Petey's Billiards, and generally lived such a normal life that it caused some people to wonder. As one friend of both families put it: "Either he is made of stone, or it hasn't struck him yet." That wise person proved to be a prophet. For, soon afterward, the full impact of it all struck Frank Dombrowski.

His personality began to change. He became melancholy, then morose. He could scarcely remember people's names. His accounting work became filled with inexcusable errors. If asked a question, he only stared back. He began to drink heavily. Then he simply refused to go to work. Refused to do anything. He would not even take a bath.

A friend who asked him, "What are you thinking about Zamyslony?" received the reply: *"Nie nazywaj mie wiecej zamyslonem, to coja prubuje nie robic, to jestmystec,"* meaning "call me 'thinking one' no longer. I am trying *not* to think." Which is about the last sensible, understandable statement Frank made. But he certainly continued to drink. The twenty or more boilermakers per day that he had been drinking for at least four weeks were a source of alarm to his friends. Such drinking would scramble a man's brains. How much longer could he take it? Also, what was he trying to prove? Suffering comes to everyone. Suffering is fine, but there must be an end to it.

And so today, in Steve Novotny's saloon, Frank Dombrowski was doing his daily routine: using alcohol as a fuel to relight, or bury, his spirit. Seeing nothing. Hearing nothing. Asking nothing. Living within himself; facing the torment within. Seeking answers to questions that always ended *why?* Why had this happened? You out there—God, or whoever you are—*why?* I *demand* an answer. If you don't give me one, expect nothing back from me. How can I go on without one? *Tell me!*

"Another boilermaker," he said to Steve Novotny on this crisp autumn morning.

"Yes, Zamyslony."

Frank made a sound deep in his throat that might have sounded like a laugh. He was thinking, Zamyslony indeed! What a farce. What shit people talk. To call me a thinking one is like calling a toilet a fountain. I know nothing. I am nothing. I believe in nothing.

And that morning, at the Drop Forge Plant, five miles away, Leo Dombrowski perspired and worked stoically at his job and grieved silently for his son. He, of all men, understood what Frank was going through. For that reason, he, the stern disciplinarian, never once criticized his son. When his wife, Sophia, wept, or his friends commiserated, Leo would say in his harsh, guttural voice, "In something like this, only time will heal. And he would add the words *"Zatosc takajak jeko-uderzy mocnego gozej jak slabszago,"* which meant that sorrow, such as his, hits the strong worse than the weak.

It was near noon now and time for Frank Dombrowski to do his daily ritual. He got up, staggered out the door, and headed towards the Holy Sepulchre Cemetery, some ten miles away, where he would visit with Valerie. And talk to her.

Aloise, after lunch, ran out to the alley on his way to school, hoping to find his brothers. But, of course, they were gone. They were at Novotny's saloon, asking about their oldest brother, Frank.

"He left twenty minutes ago," said Steve Novotny. He didn't have to explain any more than that. The brothers knew.

"How was he?" asked John.

"Not bad. Usual, I would say. He gets by the mornings pretty good cause he's got a gut like cast-iron. It's in the afternoon that it gets him. When he gets back."

The brothers said nothing. They left and returned to the alley. Sat down in almost the same spot as before. Wondering how to pass the long afternoon hours.

They didn't have to wait long. Fifteen minutes later they saw Tommy Touhy coming down the alley. There was never any doubting the identity of Touhy. He was stocky, short, and broad shouldered. He lurched along in a swaggering, barrel-gaited stride that had a certain character to it. His walk, in fact, bespoke trouble. Touhy made his entry in a typical manner: eating a banana from one hand and picking his nose with the other.

"I just saw Keltnor," he said.

The Dombrowski brothers said nothing. Indeed, they scarcely seemed to recognize his arrival, the proper code for young men at that time being one of total indifference to others.

"I just had it with Keltnor," said Touhy.

Silence.

"In fact, I just knocked Keltnor on his ass."

Again, no reaction, even though this was a proper kind of opening for a person like Touhy. The brothers were not being coy. It was never really important, or relevant, to know why Touhy knocked somebody on his ass. He was always doing it. He was an excellent street fighter who had graduated all the way to the semifinals of the AAU in the welter division. After that brief moment of glory, Tommy returned to his first love, street fighting. Keltnor was also good, but not as good as Touhy.

The long silence irked Touhy, yet he held his temper. Finally, Joseph had the decency to ask the question.

"Did you make up?"

"Sure. As soon as I knocked him on his ass, I apologized. After all, we're old friends. I bought him a beer. You know what? I think Keltnor is nuts."

"Why?"

"He says he's going on the road. He wants me to go with him."

"Why?"

"Says we might as well see the country before we settle down. Can't find a job anyhow. His old lady is driving him nuts."

John and Joseph said nothing.

"Keltnor says maybe you guys would like to go. Get five or six guys. See the west coast. Maybe Mexico. Look around before we settle down. Everyone's doin' it. You guys interested?"

Joseph glanced at his older brother. Now, at least, they knew what was on Touhy's mind. Tommy really wanted to go, and he was here for the purpose of selling them on the idea. Tommy never knew it, but he was continually getting used by Keltnor; continually getting steamed up by Keltnor's ideas. Tommy was crafty, but essentially naive, while Keltnor was both cunning and intelligent, but something of a dreamer.

John, who caught his brother's glance, knew that something had to be said on the subject of going on the road; otherwise, Tommy would never let up. He'd nag them on the subject all afternoon. And today there were more important things to worry about.

"We'll think about it," said John.

Touhy's temper flared. "You guys never can make up your mind. Someone comes up with a great idea and you can't even recognize it."

"We got other problems."

"Aw, you're both full of shit."

The brothers let that pass. Touhy sat there burning. John and Joseph were just about the two most stubborn Polacks he knew. Tell them one thing, they'd do another. It took them forever to make up their minds about anything; when they did decide, nothing could change them. He decided to find out what their problem was, and needle them. After ten minutes of relentless Irish probing, he got to the bottom of their problem: They had flagrantly disobeyed their mother, so there would be hell to pay tonight when Leo Dombrowski came home.

Tommy whistled with admiration. "Really? You just walked away like that?" He knew what old man Dombrowski's beatings were like; he had witnessed one, two years ago, when Joseph had smashed up his bicycle.

"I'll say one thing," he continued. "You guys got guts. Both of you."

Silence.

"I mean it."

"Know something else? I *agree* with you. You didn't do anything that much out of the way. Not enough to deserve no beating. After all, you're not kids no more. I wouldn't take no beating if I were you. You guys are men. Ever think of it that way? Men don't take beatings. They give 'em. Ever think of that? Listen: I respect my parents. Even though they're divorced and I don't like my stepfather. If he laid a hand on me I'd knock the shit out of him. I wouldn't even let my old man beat me, unless he could carry it through; and that I doubt; although I'd sure be bruised the next day. No sir! Not anymore. I'm a man."

"I agree," said Joseph suddenly.

John's jaw clenched. His face went red. Emotion seethed within him. There were two reasons: One, because his younger brother had spoken out of turn. This was not a decision to make lightly. Or quickly. They still had four hours before Papa came home. The second reason concerned Tommy Touhy. John wished with all his heart that Touhy had never appeared today. Tommy had put into words the very thoughts that had been forming within him. And, if he refused to take Papa's beating that night, Touhy would be the one to take all the credit. How he would gloat!

"See? Joe agrees," Touhy gloated. "How about you, Yunick?"

"I got nothing to say," said John.

"That's because you're chicken," said Touhy.

John arose slowly, and said, "You want to try and knock me on my ass?"

"No hard feelings," Touhy replied. "I was just trying to give you a little wellmeant advice. That's what friends are for, ain't they?"

He pulled a crumpled package of Wings from his pocket and offered cigarettes to both—but to Joseph first.

Sophia tried to stay out of her mother's way that day; but it was no use. Maryusha Dombrowski barked orders continuously at her fourteen-year-old daughter:

"Change the sheets."

"Wax the kitchen floor."

"Dust the blinds."

"Wash the windows."

"Vacuum the rug."

Maryusha herself took on the hardest task—cleaning the attic.

By late afternoon even Mama could think of nothing else to do. So she went to work in the kitchen, preparing *czarnina*, a delectable Polish blood soup consisting of the blood from a duck mixed with pulverized potatoes, prunes, and vinegar. Mrs. Kucinskus, her Lithuanian neighbor, dropped by and watched skeptically as Maryusha expertly slit open the neck of the duck and held it over a bowl.

"Looks good," sniffed Mrs. Kucinskus.

"Is good," Mama grunted, not particularly pleased today by the visit. Besides, they were still getting over a bitter quarrel of two weeks ago in which, Mama claimed, Mrs. Kucinskus spat in her eye.

"Enjoy it," said Mrs. Kucinskus.

"I will."

Mrs. Kucinskus left.

Aloise came home from St. Casimir's parochial school about that time. Instinctively sensing the situation, he disappeared into the basement and did not make a sound down there. Tonight's beating would surely be administered in the basement and he wanted to be where the action was. Where could he hide, he asked himself, and still miss nothing? Under the pool table? In the coal bin? No, that would not do, as it was filled with coal. Maybe the dark corner at the far end where many boxes were stored. Or under the kitchen stairs. At four-thirty the phone rang. He heard his mother answer it. Judging from her words, it was a neighbor calling to say that she had seen Frank on his way back from the cemetery and he was in bad condition.

True, or not, Mama indicated by her voice that she was not pleased with the call.

Poor Mama, thought Aloise. She was the one to feel sorry for. She had all these worries, plus today's special problem. This morning, Aloise remembered sympathizing with his brothers; but now he wasn't sure. He knew how Mama worried about Frank. How awful, he thought, that there had to be so much trouble in the world. Why couldn't everyone live in peace and happiness? Suddenly, he had a fleeting but ardent desire never to grow up. He sat there, crunched in a corner, waiting in the basement gloom for the hour of five o'clock, when Papa would come home. His heart was heavy and sad.

In the alley, time began to pass faster for the Dombrowski brothers, as Tommy Touhy, with his buoyant spirit, got them talking of the old times, the good times they had had.

"Leo Chisek," said Tommy. "Remember him?"

Of course they remembered. Who could forget Leo Chisek with his head as hard as stone; but, alas, a head that shook constantly from a nervous disorder. His Polish friends taunted him with the derisive term "Kreci Glowa," which meant "headshaker."

"That time with Chisek and Koskuski. Remember that?" Tommy asked.

They did. Alex Koskuski was also a nervous, high-strung fellow. He had a habit of spitting, not to mention a facial twitch. Alex could scarcely utter a sentence without spitting. They recalled the time Alex spotted Leo Chisek cheating Tommy Touhy in a game of pool. Tommy called Chisek "Kreci Glowa" and the fight was on. It raged the length of the pool room. Touhy hit Chisek with every punch he had, but the bull-like "headshaker" would not go down. Finally, in disgust, Touhy grabbed a pool cue—"It's not right when a guy doesn't go down. What else was I gonna do?"—and, jabbing Chisek into a corner under a sink, he began beating Leo over the head with the heavy end of the stick. Alex Koskuski objected to such tactics, and tried to lay Touhy low with a coal shovel. A free-for-all developed among fifteen others, and some serious damage was averted by the timely arrival of the Dombrowski brothers. Tommy's voice rose with the happy memories of that great fight.

"I can still see Chisek rubbing his head when I hit him with the stick. He was spitting like a cobra and yelling, 'Suffanabitch, Irisher'—he never could say sonofabitch—you don't fight fair.' Hell, how you gonna fight fair when a guy won't go down?"

Joseph chuckled and chimed in: "Yeah, he said, 'Touhy, you suffanabitch, why you hit me with pool cue,' and you said, like he owed you an apology, 'I had to, Leo. Your head's too hard.' That made him happy. 'Okay,' he said, 'you still my friend, no?'"

That brought forth the story of Ziggy Canplay and his concertina. Ziggy was an addled soul, bald at twenty, apparently homeless, who roamed the mill saloons wearing a stupid grin and playing his concertina for tips and booze.

Ziggy had no last name; at least no one had ever heard it. They knew him only as Ziggy Canplay, for whenever he saw expressions of approval as he played, he would grin widely and shout: "Ziggy can play, no?"

On one such night someone had stolen Ziggy's concertina while he was enjoying a free beer. Actually, Leo Chisek had hidden it across the street in a vacant lot. Ziggy began to cry. John Dombrowski felt sorry for the poor fellow and ordered Leo to return it. Chisek refused. The fight was on.

"You hit Chisek so hard," Tommy remembered, "he flew through the front window, and you broke a bone in your hand—remember?"

John indeed remembered. His hand had hurt for months.

"Then the cops came."

"The only one who got pinched was Ziggy Canplay because he was crawling around on his hands and knees in the lot looking for his music box. The cops thought he was drunk because he was crying like a baby."

"No, he had a box of matches. They thought he was trying to start a fire."

"Poor Ziggy. I wonder whatever happened to him?"

"I heard he got put away for indecent exposure, or rape, or something."

"Remember when we pushed coal off the trains?" This had been great sport, and an easy way to make money. Wait for a freight train as it pulled up a certain steep grade; climb aboard, and then, for the next mile, push coal off frantically. Later, they sold it for twenty-five cents a sack.

"How about the bicycle club?" said John. That was a subject that brought bad memories, especially for Tommy Touhy, who had, for a short time, been a member, although the Dombrowski brothers had never joined. The rule was that each member had to steal a bicycle a week. The parts would be interchanged and the bikes sold. The police had broken up this club; two members had been sent to St. Charles Reformatory. Tommy himself had been granted a six-month probation.

Eventually they ran out of stories. They lapsed into silence, realizing that it was getting late, and Papa soon would be home. Tommy went through his wallet, looking for a risqué card that might start conversation anew. However, sex was a subject that was taboo with the brothers. Joseph picked at a wart on his hand. John cleaned his fingernails with a piece of wire he found on the ground. Gloomily, he reflected on the crisis that lay ahead. What would he say to his father? How would he handle himself? Maybe we should run away, he brooded. Join Keltnor, Touhy, and some others. See the country. Maybe now was the time to do it. Better than being thrown out of the house, which he was sure would happen if he and Joseph stood up to their father.

The haze of industrial smoke, which always settled late in the day when there was no wind, could be seen now as dusk settled in. Spirals of soft coal smoke rose from chimneys. Down the alley, the figures of workmen could be seen trudging home with their lunch pails under their arms. The early shift at International Harvester had broken. Soon men would be walking out the gates of other industrial plants: Acme Steel, Pullman Company, Sherwin-Williams, the Calumet Shops. And, of course, the Drop Forge Plant, where Leo Dombrowski worked.

At five-twenty, the figure of Sophia Dombrowski was seen dashing out across the yard.

"Yunick! Yusiff! Pa's home!"

The brothers remained calm. Sophia seemed disappointed. "He's home!" she repeated. "He just came in."

"Don't get excited," said John. "Go back in."

"You coming in?"

"We'll come when we're ready."

"What if he asks are you here?"

"Tell him," replied John.

Sophia, still breathless, looked from one to the other. She saw Tommy Touhy and wondered what he was doing there. Tommy was such a troublemaker.

"I won't say anything," Sophia said, and returned to the house.

Slowly, John climbed to his feet and stretched his large frame. Joseph got up also.

"I'll go with you," volunteered Touhy. "All your old man can do is throw me out." Neither of the brothers objected, so Tommy trailed along as they headed for the house. They went in through the rear basement door. Without a word, the brothers began washing up at the washtub. Tommy took a cue and busied himself at the pool table.

Upstairs, the water in the bathroom could be heard running. Leo Dombrowski was also washing up. Then, his voice booming in Polish: "Are the boys home?" His tone sounded cheerful, which only made matters worse. When Papa Dombrowski had a good day, he disliked having problems dampen his spirits.

"They are downstairs," Mama Dombrowski said. "They just came in."

Nothing after that. Only foreboding silence. The brothers picked up cues and joined Touhy in making random idle shots.

Suddenly it began. Mama Dombrowski, speaking in her precise, flawless Polish, began explaining what had happened today. Her voice began to rise. *"Jac chce abys ty dal jimdo zrozumienia . . .* I want you to make them understand the meaning of such disobedience. They may be too big for me to handle, but they must do as I say, or they cannot live under this roof. Is that not right, Leo? I will have it no other way. You, Leo, have always agreed with this. Obedience was good enough for you, and for me, when we lived under our parents' roofs. . . . So must it be here. Do you agree?"

"I agree," said Leo.

"Then take what measures you must."

"Do not fear."

In the basement, Tommy Touhy began putting up his cue. "I'd better go," he said.

"No. Stay," said John.

"I may be in the way."

"Never mind. Stay!" John ordered. Touhy reluctantly picked up his cue again.

The basement door opened from upstairs. Leo Dombrowski came down with slow, measured steps.

"Yunick . . .Yusiff . . ." he called.

"Yes, Pa." The brothers put up their cues and faced their father with sullen expressions. Tommy tried to blend into the background. He whistled under his breath to show his unconcern, as he made his shots.

Leo Dombrowski was not a massive figure of a man. He was not as tall as his sons, but he was broader in the shoulders, and heavier. His arms were like steel talons, and his feats at Polish picnics were prodigious. It was said he could lift four hundred pounds without effort, which equaled the lift of some professional weight lifters.

"What's this I hear?" he asked, furrowing his black brows as he appraised his sons.

John met his father's eye and managed not to flinch. "Ma's right," he said.

"You don't mind your mother anymore? Is that it? You're too big to obey?"

Maintaining his gaze and his silence, John simply stood there. Leo turned to his younger son. "Is that right, Yusiff?"

Joseph's eyes wavered, fell, and looked away.

"Why didn't you bring in the coal on time?" Leo asked.

John's answer was respectful. "We did bring it in, Pa."

"But you didn't bring it in *on time*."

"We had something else to do first."

"Something else *first*? What does that mean? I don't understand that word 'first.' When your mother tells you to do something, you do it now. You do what you are *told*."

"Yes, Pa . . ."

Papa's voice became scathing. "I suppose you both are proud of your actions?"

Two heads bowed. John managed a monotone, "No, Pa . . ."

Leo Dombrowski sighed, almost regretfully. He advanced toward his sons. The brothers sprung backward, instantly alive to the threat. John, raising an arm instinctively in self-defense, cried out, "Wait, Pa. Don't hit us."

The impudence of such a statement caught Papa by surprise. "Why shouldn't I hit you?" He advanced another step.

"Don't hit, Pa," John cried, his tone an entreaty, his body trembling. "We're warning you."

Leo Dombrowski stopped short. His mouth fell open. "*You* are warning *me*?"

"We're not gonna take no beating, Pa."

"You *what?*" A look of utter incredulity spread over Papa's face.

"We're not gonna take it, Pa, that's all." John was breathless now. "I warn you, Pa. We're not gonna take no beating."

"And why aren't you going to take your punishment?" Leo asked, his voice deadly. "This I want to know."

"Because we don't deserve it."

"I'll decide that."

"We don't deserve it, Pa, that's all. We hauled the coal in late, but we *did* get it in. We're not gonna take no beating for that."

Papa Dombrowski stared at his sons in disbelief. His brain was reeling, unable to comprehend such mutiny. His breathing stopped. His muscles waited for the command from his brain: Which son would be first? And would he be able to control himself in the face of such rebellion? He must be careful not to permanently injure them, he warned himself. Then the thought suddenly occurred to him that perhaps the two of them were going to take him on at the same time. And, if true, maybe they could defeat him. If so, so be it. That risk had to be taken. But the *shame* of it, he thought. The *terrible* shame of it. To think that it had come to this: Father and sons fighting in the same house. His emotions tore him apart. He struggled to push them aside.

"So you're not going to take this beating?"

"We're too old for beatings, Pa. We're men, Pa."

Leo studied his sons critically, like an animal before it leaps. Suddenly, the enormity of what was he was about to do swept over him. So that's it. They are men, are they? Of course. I should have understood. What a fool he had almost been! His voice snapped out a command, "Aloise!"

Poor Aloise came out, trembling, from under the kitchen stairs, where he had been hiding all this time.

Papa pulled a bill from his pocket. "Go to the saloon. Buy a gallon of beer. A pint of whiskey. The best kind."

"Yes, Papa." Aloise scrambled out the basement door.

After that, total silence. Papa spoke no words at all. The brothers stood there, baffled and embarrassed, shifting from one foot to the other. Tommy Touhy missed a shot and muttered aloud, "Get in there, you bastard."

Soon Aloise returned, out of breath, his arms aching from the heavy bundle. Leo took it and placed it on the basement stairs.

"Aloise, get glasses!"

"Yes, Papa."

A moment later, with slow, dignified movements, Papa poured two fingers of whiskey into each of three water glasses. He handed one to each of his sons and looked at them quizzically.

"How old are you, Yunick?"

"Nineteen."

"And you, Yusiff?"

"Eighteen."

"Both of you are too old for beatings, is that it? Ready for the world. So be it. All right. From now on, you are no longer boys. No longer to be treated like boys. *You are men!* Now begins the time when you must *live* and *act* like men. You know what that means?"

"Yes sir."

"That means to live in honor; to do *honor* to one's family, to one's country, to those you work with; to accept responsibility. Understand?"

"Yes sir."

"All right, then. A toast to your position as men in this world. You have all the responsibility that goes with that word. Never again a beating. But, take *care* never to *dishonor me or my house.* Is that clear?"

"Yes."

"Then drink." He touched his glass to theirs and downed his whiskey.

"Now then," said Papa, still solemn, but smiling faintly, "see if you can finish the rest of this bottle, like men, and not get drunk doing it. There is nothing finer than good whiskey, if one knows how to handle it. If your friend is also a man, give him a drink." With that, Leo Dombrowski turned and marched upstairs with dignity.

"Jesus!" Tommy Touhy exclaimed. "Hurry up and give me that drink. I need it." Touhy poured himself *three* fingers into the glass Papa had used, and gulped it down. He wiped the sweat off his brow. "What a man!"

The Dombrowski brothers looked far from victorious. They looked, instead, crushed. Defeated. Engulfed with shame, remorse, and guilt. So now they were men. How would they ever live up to the responsibilities their father had placed upon them? How could they ever live up to the *name* of Leo Dombrowski? Taking a beating would have been far more preferable.

At the table that night, the *czarnina* was excellent. In fact, the entire meal was good, although, judging from the subdued mood of the family, one might think the meal was bad. It was just that so much happened that day, everyone was emotionally exhausted. Each member—except Frank, who was not home—needed time, isolation, to sort out his thoughts. Aloise, for some reason, could not keep his eyes off of his brothers. Why, if they had escaped a beating and were now men, did they look so unhappy?

Conversation was brief and desultory. Mama mentioned that Mrs. Kucinskus had visited today and showed interest in the blood soup. Leo said that there had been an accident at the plant today. A man had lost his hand.

"Whose fault was it?" Maryusha asked.

"His own. We have good safety precautions at the plant. He's lucky he didn't lose an arm."

When Mama was in the kitchen getting coffee and Sophia was clearing the table, Sophia mentioned that someone had called in the afternoon to tell about Frank.

Leo slapped the table. "That's gossip, Zoshka! Who cares about that? You should be ashamed of yourself."

"I just said . . ."

"Keep your silly tongue in your silly head. We know about Frank. Who needs to tell us?"

Sophia blushed and retreated to the kitchen to help her mother. That made matters worse. The mere mention of Frank's name brought forward the pall that was always waiting in the background.

Leo lit his pipe and puffed it as the coffee was being served. After a long silence, he said, "Frank is a good man. His sorrow is deep. But he will be all right."

Maryusha looked up expectantly. "Of course," she agreed. "Of course. *Boze blogoslaw go*," which meant, God bless him.

"Ah, yes," said Leo. "I agree."

Just then the front door opened. It was Frank coming home. They heard his fumbling in the vestibule. He had difficulty climbing the stairs, and sounded very drunk indeed.

The family listened in dread, following his every movement with their ears. They heard him staggering around in the upstairs bedroom. An object crashed. A curse. Then the thud of his body as it missed the bed and fell to the floor.

Maryusha gave a little cry and jumped up. Leo raised his hand.

"Leave him alone. He'll be all right."

Maryusha sat down. She seemed unconscious of the tears that rolled down her cheeks. Her hands clutched the napkin so tightly that her knuckles showed white. Yet she sat very straight, with a kind of dignity that was poignant and awesome.

"*Boze blogoslaw go,*" she murmured again.

Leo Dombrowski sighed and relit his pipe. He glanced toward the ceiling. The others looked at him, to him, for the words that would make everything all right, or at least a little better.

"Yes indeed," he said, "*Boze blogoslaw go.* All he needs is time. For him, each day time is passing, and that is good. I have faith in my son. He will be *all right.* I promise you."

Jesus Tramped through Jerusalem

It was safe now and they could come out of the reefer. Three travelers heading east across New Mexico: Swanson, Koko, and Keltnor. But it had been rough back there at Tularosa. Worse than Alamogordo. Things were getting worse in the mid-thirties.

Tularosa, of all place. Little more than a wide spot in the middle of the road. A water tower, a Shell gas station, and maybe three hundred people. The water tower was for the town, not the train. Freights had no reason to stop there, but this one did.

In Alamogordo it was bad enough, no question about that. But then, one expected things to be bad in Alamogordo. The transient camp in an old garage at the edge of town housed and fed a changing population of at least a hundred itinerants who were trying to "get through" the roadblock that the railroad bulls had set up. Every day a brave, or foolhardy, dozen or so would make the attempt. And why not? Why not try the East? They had already tried the West. They had drifted through Arizona, Nevada, Texas; not to mention California, the state they bitterly called "the land of milk and honey." Everywhere back *there* it was monotonously the same—*bad*.

In Alamogordo, the word was that the checkpoint at the other end of the Southern Pacific line was Tucumcari, 230 miles east. Every day a few tried to get through, while the smart ones, the timid ones, and the cautious ones waited to see how many actually got through. Usually, if a dozen tried, eleven came back bloody and beaten. Some with faces that were scarcely recognizable, others bruised and limping, always one or two with broken bones or fractures. The railroads said they hadn't hired the bulls—the insurance companies were the culprits. They were unhappy with losses on freight trains. They had set up roadblocks on freight lines throughout the land. The word spread quickly. Those who were unfortunate enough to run into one said the bulls had to be given credit for their efficiency. They knew how to do their jobs. They could shake down a one-hundred-ten-car freight train in less than half an hour. They knew every trick in the book. Some adventurous travelers even resorted to riding the rods under the cars, a dangerous and antiquated way of traveling. But the bulls were checking the rods also, along with the reefers, the open boxcars, the oil tankers, the flatbed cars, and the coal gondolas. They had an uncanny knack for digging travelers out from under coal. They flushed every nook and cranny of flat cars loaded with steel, lumber, auto frames, and industrial parts. They missed nothing.

It was not a good time, that year, to move through the Land of the Free. And yet the papers said five million people were on the move. Never had the natives been so restless. The real hoboes were hopelessly outnumbered. And flattered. Never had they so much company, and such quality of company. Along with the bindlestiffs, crop workers, and shareholders, there were respectable farmers who had been foreclosed or ruined by draught and dust storms, respectable families from cities and villages; women nursing babies in boxcars were a common sight. And there were the young: college kids out for a summer lark; tough kids from city ghettos—from the 42 Gang in Chicago, and the Purple Gang from Detroit. It was, that summer, the largest migration from No Place to Nowhere that America had ever seen. As one kid put it to Keltnor: "I'm a product of the alphabet. We live under NRA. My old man worked for WPA. I'm in the CCC. And I still have trouble with my ABCs."

After the bulls shook down the freight a second time at Tularosa and the train had been rolling a few miles, the three young men dared to come out of the reefer, a deep, rectangular refrigerator compartment that could be either a safe, warm refuge from the weather or a tomb. You never dropped into a reefer compartment alone, because the drop was more than eight feet and there was no way to get out. Reefers were safe only for two or more. Even then it had its dangers. Sometimes the bulls, as they walked the roofs of the cars, slammed the hatches shut and locked them. There was no way to get out of a locked reefer. Also, they were soundproof. Standing in a freight yard in a locked reefer, you could shout your lungs out and no one would hear you. Ten days and three thousand miles later, the hatch might be opened for "icing." But the car could lay on a siding for sixty days or longer—a guaranteed way of losing weight.

Keltnor and Koko hoisted Swanson up the corrugated sides of the compartment. The hatch had not been locked. Swanson raised it and surveyed the scene with extraordinary caution. At last, he pushed the hatch open all the way and pulled himself up and out. Koko followed, and the two then pulled Keltnor out.

Systematically, they cased the train again, even though they had done so after getting through the roadblock at Alamogordo. Casing was important and necessary. You had to know what options you had in the cars ahead and behind:

How many open reefers were there; how many tank cars, flat cars, and gondolas; where could you hide if the bulls came while the train was rolling? A bull—even a pair of them—would think twice about taking on more than one traveler; unless, of course, the bull was armed. Then the decision was quickly made. A shot in the air, or close to one's head, and the wise traveler debarked over the side with no questions asked, even at speeds of sixty miles an hour.

The three of them picked a spot two-thirds down the length of the train. The farther back, the better—less soot and cinders from the coal-burning engine. Yet not too far back, especially if there is a moon, because your silhouette can be detected by the brakeman, or bulls, if they are riding caboose.

The moon was only in its second quarter tonight, yet it cast enough light to cause them to move forward until they were at about the midway point.

Swanson gave a short, humorless chuckle. "Damned if I can understand it."

"Understand what?"

"First Alamogordo. Then Tularosa. And we get through. Koko, you must be the lucky one."

"Not me," said Koko, who was black, tall, and in his late teens. "I never brought nobody good luck."

"Then it must be you, Keltnor."

Keltnor said nothing. It was sufficient now just to relax and enjoy their luck. Such opportunities did not come often on the road. You were always tense about something. And if you weren't tense, you were miserable with the cold or rain, or drenched with perspiration in some closed boxcar filled with straw and horse manure. Right now, it was quite enough just to sit there and let the warm, dry, desert air cool your skin, and look up at the moon, and feel the rhythm of the wheels, and the gentle swaying motion of the train. A freight, when it runs at the proper speed—under fifty miles an hour—can be as enjoyable as being at sea.

Swanson took off his dirty T-shirt and scratched himself. His body was covered with the dark purple splotches of impetigo. "Sure beats my ass how we made it," he said.

"I can still see that guy getting it from that bull back in Alamogordo," said Koko. "That blackjack coming down across his shoulder blade. I think I heard the bone crack."

Swanson laughed. He had a rare sense of humor.

None of them had known each other very long. Only since Alamogordo, where they slept on adjacent mattresses on the concrete garage floor, ate their daily rations of salami and hard rolls, and exchanged lies with each other. Swanson claimed to be a dirt-track driver from Pennsylvania. To hear him tell it, he once had a tryout at Indianapolis, but had been "shafted" by another driver who had it in for him. Hearing Swanson's lies did not bother Keltnor. Everyone lied. Lying was about the only dignity anyone had on the road.

Koko's story was that he had busted out of a CCC camp in Utah. Strangely enough, Koko did not have many lies to tell. He was "deep down lonely," he said, and was on his way back home to his family in Detroit. "What there is left of the family," he told Keltnor one day at the transient camp. "I don't know if my father is there anymore. He's been out of work for so long, I got a feeling he done up and pulled out. Nobody has written me a letter for three months."

Swanson stretched and yawned. "Sure feels good."

"Sure do," said Koko.

"Hey, Keltnor, think you'll ever amount to anything?" Swanson laughed. This was one of Swanson's favorite jokes. He had asked Keltnor that question a dozen times during their four days in Alamogordo. But he never asked Koko the question. He treated Koko with condescension. Keltnor, being white, was his equal, and he treated all of his equals with a peculiar kind of arrogance. Swanson definitely had a chip on his shoulder.

"How far you figure it is to Tucumcari?" Swanson asked after a while.

"About 215 miles."

"We got about five hours to relax."

"Won't have any trouble at Tucumcari. Might ride right on through."

Swanson was probably right about that, Keltnor thought. The checkpoint at Tucumcari was set up to stop the hordes heading west, not to stop the lucky few who got past Alamogordo and Tularosa; although, these days, you never could be sure. The bulls were learning so many fancy tricks—like the second shakedown at Tularosa. What purpose had that served, wondered Keltnor, except to knock off one or two miserable bastards who would have to walk all the way to Tucumcari? In the daytime, with the heat hitting one hundred, you got the feeling you were getting a preview of hell.

After ten minutes, Swanson became talkative. "If we only had a broad," he said. "Hey, wouldn't that be great? I never laid a broad on top of a freight. Laid 'em plenty inside cars. Some didn't like it too much, but if you squeeze 'em around the throat, they get the idea. Then they just lay there and take it. They won't admit it, but they really like it that way." He chuckled at the pleasant memories. The others said nothing.

"Hey, Koko, you ever lay a white broad?"

"No."

"Why not? I've laid colored broads. They're pretty good. Had one in Tijuana, but I think I got the clap from her. 'Course, I couldn't tell exactly who gave it to me, I had so many down there."

Keltnor and Koko listened as Swanson rambled on. Normally, he was taciturn, but he became almost garrulous whenever he talked about sex or auto racing. It was alright listening to Swanson this time, thought Keltnor. His lies were not as irritating as they usually were. Being hunched down under the second quarter moon, feeling the warm desert air wash over them, made everything right. Nothing Swanson said could make much difference. Then Swanson lapsed into moody silence. He kept still for a long time.

"I tell you one thing," he said suddenly. "Ain't gonna be that way no more. Goin' back to Pennsylvania, get a car and start driving dirt tracks again. Know a guy who's got a new Offy. Said he'd give me a shot at it. This time there ain't gonna be no booze or broads. They're the worst two things a guy can get into. Gonna settle down. I see other guys makin' it. No reason I can't. How 'bout you, Koko. What you gonna do?"

"Told you, I'm goin' home."

"What you gonna do when you get there?"

"Dunno. Look 'round for a job, I guess."

"In Detroit? How you gonna get a job in Detroit? Shit, man, there ain't no jobs in Detroit. Everybody knows that."

"Can't find a job, maybe I'll go back to the Cs."

"How you gonna get back in? You already ran away

from one camp. They won't let you back in."

"Might be, I'll join the Army."

"Shit, man, you won't get in no Army. Navy neither. Even a white man can't get in. They got them quotas. Only take a few each month."

Koko said nothing. He was thinking that maybe Swanson was right. But just now he couldn't be bothered. No, it was good just to sit here and enjoy being alive.

Swanson leaned forward suddenly. "Hey! Somebody's coming!"

"Where?"

"Heading this way from the caboose."

Koko and Keltnor strained their eyes trying to pierce the darkness. All they could see was the pale green light on the caboose half a mile away. Maybe Swanson *had* been a race driver, if he could see that good.

"Tell ya, somebody's coming. Ain't you guys got eyes?"

Now they could see. There was the faint outline of a body about twenty cars away. And he was coming closer. All three flattened on their stomachs to reduce their profile.

"Shall we spread out?"

"No, stay like we are. Don't think he's seen us yet. Lay low."

The figure gradually grew larger. It's outline now was plainly visible. Whoever it was, he wasn't large. When he was about six cars away, Koko asked: "Is it a bull?"

"Can't tell. Lay low."

"He hasn't seen us yet."

"No, but he will."

On he came, walking slowly, relaxed, looking in their direction. Four cars away.

Not until he was one car away did the stranger spot

them. He stopped in the midst of a stride. And froze.

"He's seen us!"

"Yeah. He's just standing there."

Now came the critical time. If he was a bull, he would do one of two things: go back for more help, or, if he had a gun, advance.

Surprisingly, the stranger did neither. He merely stood there, absolutely motionless. Then, to the amazement of the three, he turned around, and again stood there, looking back toward the caboose.

"It's not a bull," said Swanson.

"How you know? He raised his arms. Maybe he's giving a signal."

"Nobody could see that far from the caboose. He's just another 'bo."

Keltnor thought that Swanson probably was right. The stranger looked too short to be a bull. He was fat. Probably just another 'bo traveling alone. But how had he gotten through? Keltnor was convinced that he, Swanson, and Koko were the only ones who had gotten through.

Swanson could stand the suspense no longer. "Gonna check him out. You guys wait here." He stood up and walked cautiously toward the stranger. Koko and Keltnor watched as Swanson reached the stranger and tapped him on the shoulder. The stranger scarcely paid attention. He raised his arms again and seemed to be pointing to some point in the sky. Swanson stood there, apparently listening to him.

Finally, Swanson returned. Shaking his head in disbelief. "That guy's crazy. He's completely off his rocker."

"What did he do?"

"He's got on a preacher's hat. He's *preaching!*"

"What?"

"Yeah! Waving his arms around like a gooney bird. Pointing out there. Man, he gave me the creeps. I had to get out of there. Know what else he did?"

"What?"

"He gave me his *blessing*! He put his hand on me and said, 'I am the Son of the Son. Bless you. Peace shall be with you.'"

"Jesus!" said Koko.

"He said something about great music out there. He asked me if I could hear it. I told him, 'Sure, I can hear it. It sounds great.' Then I hauled my ass out of there. What a nut!"

Koko laughed and got up. "I'm gonna get his blessing, too." With that, he got up and walked the half car length to the end of the car, jumped across to the next car, and walked midway to where the stranger stood. He was a fat, paunchy little guy with a broad face that was covered by a wide-brimmed Quaker hat. Koko tapped him on the shoulder.

"Good evening, son," said the stranger.

"Who are you?"

"Don't you know who I am?"

"That's why I asked."

"I am the Son of the Son."

"Yeah. Sure. I'm the Wandering Jew."

Suddenly the stranger seemed to have a seizure. He began flapping his arms and writhing as though he were in pain.

"Can't you hear it out there? Such beautiful music! The sounds! Hear them? The symphony of Creation. I feel it all. Hear it all. The beauty is too much to behold. Its radiance is dazzling. See and hear with me, my son, and you shall be saved."

All Koko could hear was the rhythm of the wheels on cold steel, and the gentle caress of the desert breeze. All he could see was the green light on the caboose.

"All of you listen now," continued the stranger. "Harken to what I say. Jesus tramped through Jerusalem, do you hear me? Yes, he did. Oh yes! Who sayeth nay to that? He tramped the hills of Judea. Why shouldn't I, His Son, tramp through America? Spreading His word. His spirit. Who sayeth nay to that?"

The stranger waited, as though for a response. Apparently no one said nay, and he went on, ignoring Koko now. Koko tapped his arm.

"Hey, old man, how about a blessing?

The stranger turned and placed a hand on Koko's head: "Go in peace, my son. You have my blessing. No harm shall come to you. Go hear, listen to the divine symphony of life. There's great music out there. Miss none of it. . . ."

Koko returned to his friends. "You're right. He's really gone. Hang around him long enough and you begin hearing things."

"Did he give you his blessing?"

"Sure did. Don't I look better?"

Swanson roared. "Why didn't you tell him to change your color, Koko? Then you'd really be blessed."

"Up your ass, Swanson."

Swanson took no offense. He was too amused by the goofy preacher. "What gets me is, how did that bastard ever get through those two roadblocks? You guys ever think of that?"

They did now. And both laughed. Maybe it was a miracle, they said. Maybe the old guy just zoomed down from the sky. Or maybe he made himself invisible when the bulls came.

"He probably gave those bulls his blessing and they were so dumbfounded they couldn't swing their zappers."

Keltnor's curiosity got the best of him. He stood up and announced, "I'm gonna get my blessing, too."

"Sure, Keltnor. Everybody's gotta get blessed. Don't cost nothing."

Keltnor left, and returned a few minutes later.

"Did you get his blessing?" asked Swanson.

"I got it. Maybe he's not so crazy after all."

"What do you mean?"

"He *does* hear things out there. Just because we can't hear them, doesn't mean he's crazy. Maybe we're the crazy ones."

"What the hell you talking about, Keltnor?"

"Don't know. Just said maybe."

Swanson spit with the wind in disgust. "Keltnor, you're full of shit."

"Maybe," said Keltnor.

Keltnor's words had a sobering effect on the others. They sat there in silence for a long while. Then, suddenly, Swanson exploded, his voice filled with angry emotion.

"I tell you, that S.O.B.'s crazy! He should be put on a funny farm. Better yet, he should be put out of his misery. And I'm just the guy who can do it."

"What do you mean?"

"A guy like that shouldn't be allowed to run around loose. One little push and his troubles would be over."

Swanson made no move. He sat there glowering, seething inside. Keltnor could feel it. Why is he so upset? Keltnor wondered. Something deep inside was eating at him. And poor Christ, Keltnor mused. Christ had lasted about thirty years in His time. If he were tramping through America these days, he's probably get strung up before he could get from Los Angeles to New York.

Then Swanson lashed out again:

"Koko, why the hell did you do it?"

"Do what?"

"Go ask that S.O.B. for his blessing."

Koko was puzzled. "I don't know. I went 'cause you went, I guess."

"You dumb bastard! I didn't ask for no blessing. He *gave* it to me. I just went to see what kind of a screwball he was."

"Okay." Koko gave a little laugh. "Hell, I'll take any man's blessing. Who knows who's got the right number?"

Keltnor said he agreed. Koko had a point, he mused. In these times, who had the right, or the courage, *not* to believe? Maybe some day we would be so self-sufficient, so sure of ourselves, we wouldn't have to believe in *anything*. Maybe that would be good, and maybe it wouldn't. Swanson's problem was that he wanted to believe and couldn't. How that preacher got past those bulls at Alamogordo and Tularosa—that was the problem that bothered Swanson.

"Hey, Keltnor," said Swanson after a while, "answer me one question: Why *did* you go back there and ask for his blessing?"

"Don't know. I went because I went."

That ended it. Swanson became mute. He moved away from both of them to a new position, on his belly, and lay there, letting his emotions run down.

After a while, Koko said to Keltnor, "You know something, Keltnor?"

"What, Koko?"

"It ain't exactly like I said. It ain't exactly that I'm lonely just for my family. That's just part of it. Know what I mean? What I mean is, I'm just lonely, period. You understand?"

Keltnor said he thought he did.

"I'm lonely 'cause I just don't seem to know where I gonna fit in. What I gonna do. Where I gonna do it." Keltnor tried to reassure him, but Koko shook his head and said that he just didn't know.

"Have you given up, Koko?"

Koko thought for a long time. His words came slowly and with agonizing uncertainty. "No, I don't guess I given up yet. Wouldn't want to do that. Seem like that makes it worse. Figure I'll fit in someplace. Somewhere. Something gonna come along where I can fit. Keep tellin' myself that."

The two disengaged after that. There was no more to say. They turned inward, became islands unto themselves.

All three were islands now, each lost in his own world, hunched down, facing backward toward the past, while the train propelled them forward to a future they did not know. The preacher was facing backward, too. All four sat there motionless, rigid, as though transfixed by thoughts of the fate that awaited them; by the magic, and the awe, and the terror, and the mystery of being alive in the imponderable universe.

Gargoyles

Eight strangers crouched before the fire, sneaking hostile glances at each other, asking themselves: Who could they blame for the predicament they were in? Who had goofed? Who had jumped off first, back there at Blackfoot, causing the others to follow, like sheep, scrambling across to another track to catch a slow-moving freight heading, they thought, toward Pocatello, where they should have been hours ago, instead of this forsaken spot in the wilderness of central Idaho?

On the fine edge of Nowhere, that's where they were, in the middle of the night with a northern wind freshening. Only mid-October, and the first storm of the winter was on its way. Their only link with civilization was the trestle bridge over the United Pacific track three hundred yards away, five miles north of Arco.

Arco, of all places. They were heading north again, instead of south, toward Salt Lake City, and eventually California. The spur in the wrong direction ended at Mackay, twenty-six miles further north, where it simply stopped. There, civilization itself virtually stopped.

So who was the sonofabitch that goofed back there at Blackfoot, they were thinking, after such good progress all day long from Missoula? Not that they had been a group on the way down. They were eight strangers, eight separate bodies, eight separate heads, peering out from eight differ-ent boxcars in the darkness at Blackfoot. They were looking for signs—a water tower with a name on it, a sign on a building indicating the name of the town—when someone near the front of the train had jumped off. The others immediately followed. In two minutes, the scramble was over, everyone securely aboard the new freight, lodged in separate cars. Then, an hour later, passing through the first town, and one much too small to be Pocatello, they spotted the word "Arco" on a water tower. Their worst suspicions confirmed: Arco was sixty miles north of Blackfoot. To add a touch of irony, the train rattled through Arco at forty miles an hour. They couldn't get off until the train hit a steep grade five miles out of town. Finally, at the trestle, which spanned a treacherous ravine, it slowed down enough for each to tumble off, pick himself up, and begin the nagging, bitter question: Who was the sonofabitch that goofed?

They sat there now before the fire, hating each other and themselves with fine impartiality; feeling the dark, foreboding cliffs and mountain crags of the upper Wasatch Range; listening for sounds on the other side of the wind: the sound of their neighbors—mountain lions, wolves, coyotes, black bears, deer, elk, moose, cougars, and bobcats—not to mention timber rattlers.

Two black hoboes. A Mexican. A burly Irishman. A young man, frightened. A grinning fellow, his mouth fixed in a malevolent half-smile, his eyes darting from face to face, looking for strength or weakness in the others. Two large, brooding white men, fixing their eyes on the fire. The Irishman walked off into the forest. "To piss," he had explained. But he disappeared too many times for that. He came back now, wiping his lips, staggering.

"Alright," he said. "Who was it?"

No one answered.

"Who is the sonofabitch with guts enough to admit he

was the first one off that train back at Blackfoot?"

Silence.

"If I knew who it was, I'd kill him."

"I would help you," said the grinning man.

"You would?"

"Yes."

"Shit. Wouldn't need your help. Do it myself."

"Wasn't me," said the Mexican.

"Not me," said one of the blacks.

"I know who it was," said the Irishman.

Keltnor felt his heart plunge to his stomach. He was sure he'd been the one who had jumped off first. Only because he was too cold to cling to the outside of that reefer any longer. If he went another mile he was sure he would fall off. All he wanted to do was find someplace where he could get warm—the police station was usually the best place to go. But then, on another track, he had seen the other train pulling out. It had numerous open boxcars—which made it a different story. The inside of a boxcar could be tolerably warm, especially if there was straw, paper, or any kind of debris on the floor. He grabbed an empty, while the others followed, grabbing other empties. Keltnor wasn't sure if he had been the first one on the second train, but he was sure he had been the first one off the first train. And the Irishman had seen him.

He felt the drunk's angry gaze and wondered if the others were suspicious of him. Not yet. They stared into the fire, brooding over their rotten luck, listening to the wind as it sang a dirge through the tall pines.

Suddenly a cry pierced the air. A blood-curdling sound, very close. Baleful. A witch's cry.

"Bloodhounds!" someone said.

Again they heard it. Sad and prolonged. A lament to the

fate of all living creatures; a century away, yet close enough to reach out and touch.

"No," said the Irishman. He stood up, cursed into the darkness, and stalked off, mumbling something about choking a few coyotes.

Keltnor shivered and had a quick dialogue with himself. Under the circumstances, it made absolutely no sense to remain where he was. Common sense demanded that he put this group behind him without further delay.

But where would he go? Nothing could convince him to go off into that forest alone. Nothing would convince him that the bears and mountain lions out there would not attack him. And if he left the fire, he might freeze to death. The train coming back tomorrow from Mackay was undoubtedly the only train back. He had to be on that.

He caught the grinning one panning him slowly with his small, black eyes. He struck Keltnor as a little mad, a soul possessed of mischievous devils, all crying for utterance. He seemed as though he knew something the rest did not know—a secret, perhaps, that they were seeking, but that he would not reveal until they paid the price. What price?

All at once, a thought came to Keltnor: a connection. He remembered reading a piece in a paper a week or so ago—was it in Spokane or Missoula? He could not remember. The story told of some prisoners who had escaped from a penitentiary somewhere in Montana. Could this be their delegation? If so, he was a definite liability to them. The Irishman might not be kidding. He thought of his carcass furnishing tidbits to cougars.

A crackling noise brought several of the men to their feet. Keltnor tried, but was too paralyzed to move. It was only the Irishman returning, surlier than before. Seeing their fear, he let out a big laugh.

"There's activity out there," he said. "Lots of it."

"What kinds?"

"All kinds. And I know the sonofabitch that did it."

"Did what?"

"Led us into this trap."

"Shut up!" cried one of the men. "There ain't no trap."

The Irishman got the message. "Okay. Ain't no trap. We're stuck here till tomorrow. That's all."

"Yes. That's all."

"We catch the train going back tomorrow."

"That's right."

Suspicion turned on the Irishman. "What you doin' goin' out there all the time?" one of the blacks demanded.

The Irishman laughed and spat into the fire. "Because I don't like you sonsofbitches. Gotta get away from you sonsofbitches. You're bad news. All of ya's." He sat down, and as he did, Keltnor saw the reason for his frequent excursions: a pint bottle sticking out of his pocket, less than half full. No wonder he had so much courage, Keltnor thought. There was nothing so courageous—or foolhardy—as an Irishman with liquor in his belly.

Someone else also spotted the bottle, and asked, "What you got there?"

"Where?"

"In your back pocket."

"None of your damned business."

"Share it."

"Share what?"

"What you got in that bottle."

The Irishman tossed back his shaggy head and roared. "That's cough syrup. I got a cold."

"We all got a cold."

He liked that, and laughed again. "Not like I got. Hey, kid, you got a cold?"

Keltnor promptly said yes and noted the fact that none of them seemed to have names. Which meant they *had* to be a group. He watched the Irishman studying the others, measuring the danger: How *badly* did they want him to share that bottle?

"I believe in sharing," he said after a while. "At the right time."

"This is the right time."

"I'll decide that."

"No. *We'll* decide that."

The grinning one stood up. "The time is now."

"Sit down before I kill you."

One of the blacks stood up.

"You too," said the Irishman.

The black man sat down. It was, indeed, the right time. But they lost it. The Irishman had won—for the moment. All the others could do was wait. But collectively, they had not lost. They would wait a little longer. The next move was up to the Irishman.

When the Mexican threw a piece of wood onto the fire, the flames leaped. The others let its magic capture them, and scarcely noticed as the Irishman, now morose, stood up and stalked off into the trees.

Several minutes later he returned, growling again with laughter, perhaps to signal his return. He dangled the bottle before them, his expression self-righteous.

"I share because I want to share, not because you sonsofbitches say so. Here. Warm your guts with what I had the brains to provide."

He passed the bottle and it made the rounds, each one

taking passionate swigs, them shaking his head in shock at the horrible taste of the rotgut whiskey. Keltnor sat there appalled at what was going on, for he alone knew what had happened. The bottle had been half empty when first he had spotted it; when the Irishman had stalked off a moment ago, and returned, it was three-quarters full. There could be only one conclusion: The Irishman had pissed into it. The others were drinking a one-third mixture of urine! When Keltnor's turn came, he reacted compulsively, his mind unable to compute any other action. With a movement as swift as an adder, he tossed the remainder of the whiskey in the Irishman's face.

Then he ran.

Through the forest, crashing into fallen logs, stumbling, falling, getting up again, and running on and on until he was exhausted, but knew he was safe. Safe from *them*. But not from the alien world that now owned his soul. *Bears won't bother you. Mountain lions have to be attacked. Cougars are cowards. The rattlers are underground. You're perfectly safe in the Rockies.* Bullshit. He'd heard all that before—and believed it then. But now no power on earth could make him believe it. He *felt* that animal world out there. He knew that hundreds of hostile eyes were out there peering at him—hungry, evil, malevolent.

An hour later, he crept back, preferring the known enemy over the unknown. Twenty yards away, he lay there shivering, watching the group crouched before the fire. The fire did strange things to their faces. Mad grotesques of light and shadow made them look scarcely like faces at all, but more like gargoyles.

What a City Is

Benjamin "Slats" Ross was quite a guy. He was tall and skinny, his pants held up by suspenders as high as his chest. He worked at Western Union because that, he said, was where the action was. He was night manager of the Manhattan branch on Broadway and Forty-fourth, and Keltnor had met him during one of his frequent stranded periods when he was sending wires, collect, to his family and friends, begging for money. Keltnor wasn't fussy about whom he wired. His mother was occasionally good for five dollars, but not often. Her stock reply lately was: go into a Civilian Conservation Camp like other healthy boys and do something useful. Keltnor would then pull out his list and send wires to uncles, aunts, cousins, and anyone he could remotely call a friend.

Slats Ross liked to talk. Born and reared in New York City, he would ramble on in vague, mysterious terms about all the living he had done. Keltnor didn't think he had done much living at all, but one thing Keltnor had to admit: Slats Ross was a man of ideas.

One idea Slats had was about cities. He hated cities, he said, but now where you going to go to escape them? He wore spats along his high pants. He did the lindy hop on Saturday night at Roseland, and attended the Roxy whenever the bill changed. On Sundays, he indulged in the one gourmet meal per week he could afford on his salary of fifteen dollars a week. He ate at Jack Dempsey's and had the best on the menu for a dollar seventy-five.

How Slats could manage to remain so cheerful and confident during these hard times, Keltnor never could understand. The Depression couldn't last forever, said Slats, and when it was over, he was going to get his. He was quite knowledgeable about the stock market and invested "pretend" money on a daily basis. His specialty was selling short, and the summer of 1935, he had made, on paper, thirty-seven thousand dollars.

"It's all going to end soon, then watch this country go," Slats would say.

"Go where?" Keltnor would ask.

Slats didn't quite know. This was a time when General Motors was on strike; twenty-five percent of the labor force was still out of work; kids were fighting to get into the CCCs because the Army, Navy, and Marine quotas always seemed filled; dislocated families were riding freights through dust storms in the West. Not that Keltnor himself felt exactly depressed. He was young and getting by, taking it all in, and wondering where it would end.

That summer night, as they strolled along Broadway amusing themselves by looking at the various theater marquees—Jean Harlow was playing in *Dinner at Eight*; Clark Gable was playing in *It Happened One Night*; Eleanor Powell in *Born to Dance*—Slats began explaining his idea about cities.

A city was like a desert without an oasis, Slats said. The tall, angular buildings were not skyscrapers. They were "grotesques of steel," and they pulsated with a kind of "anamorphic life" that was beyond belief. The people imprisoned in these steel and concrete grotesques were worse than robots. They were really "formless bits of protoplasm" who appeared periodically and moved aimlessly through the streets, compelled, hypnotized by a dreadful antilife force, and then were swallowed up again in the grotesques of steel.

"That's what a city is," Slats concluded.

"You read too much," said Keltnor. "If that's what a city is, why don't you do something about it?"

"Can't. It's too late."

"You can leave it."

"Where can I go? I'm one of the robots myself. I'm caught in the trap with the others. We've lost the true vision of life. It's too late.

"We're all doomed," Slats continued, chewing intently on fragrant bits of Sen-Sen. "It's too bad. A long time ago, things got out of hand. We got too big for our britches. Now we're paying the price. The only thing to do is blow up all the cities and start over."

"You sound like an anarchist."

"I am. Do you know I'm a card-carrying Communist? YCL. Know what that means?"

"No."

"Young Communist League. Wanna see my card?"

"They all look alike."

"It's right here in my wallet. But I don't go to meetings anymore. They talk too much. All talk and no action. They're full of shit. Besides, they're against the profit motive. I used to be, too, but I decided it's too late to be against that. Who's gonna change the world now? The pattern is set. The die is cast. Besides, I don't have enough character to be Commie. I'm too selfish. I'm going out to make mine along with the rest. If it's dog eat dog, I'm gonna do the eating."

They stopped off at Child's and had coffee and rolls for two, for a nickel. Slats said, "You think I'm kidding? You come with me. I'll show you what I mean by cities."

Back to the Western Union office they went. It was 11:45 on Saturday night. Music blared and there was laughter in the air. The theaters were breaking and the sidewalks were jammed. When they got to Forty-fourth Street, Slats said, "You sit down where I tell you, inside the railing. Sit on the bench with the messengers, and watch. I'll tell you what to look for."

Keltnor did as he was told, figuring that this was as good a place as any to wait for answers to his telegrams. He had sent six that afternoon, and if he got lucky, maybe there'd be a wire, with money, before the place closed.

After a few minutes, an old man came in. Slats said, "Watch him closely."

He was very old and rather feeble, but he had a certain dignity about him. The old fellow settled himself inconspicuously in a corner near the wastebasket. He took a pad of telegram forms and pretended to be writing a message, except that he didn't write. This was only a cover-up. Every few minutes he would cast a furtive glance in both directions, then bend down as if to tie his shoes. But instead, he would reach into the wastebasket and pull out a handful of crumpled telegraph forms which had been discarded by senders who had filled them with practice messages. These he would carefully, secretively stuff into his pockets.

After a while, his pockets full, he turned and walked out.

Slats led Keltnor to the door, where they watched him go across the street. He was soon lost in the crowd.

"See that window up there?" Slats pointed to a cheap

hotel a block away. "That's his room. In a few minutes, his light will go on."

"How do you know where he lives?"

"I followed him once."

Sure enough, a few minutes later, a feeble yellow gleam appeared in the window.

"Okay," said Keltnor. "I give up. Who put the overalls in Mrs. Murphy's chowder?"

"I'll explain it to you," said Slats. His theory was that the old man was dying of loneliness. He was one of those robots living in a grotesque of steel. He was reading those messages right now, tenderly smoothing them out on his bed.

Jerry dying. Come home at once.

Sell stock at 22. Don't care what Jack says.

Broke and Hungry. Send money if can.

To sweetest girl of all. Am flying San Francisco. Understand everything.

The old man's excitement would mount. His pulse would race. He was returning, if only briefly, to the living. After all, he had no one else. But no, that was wrong. He had many. He was necessary to many. He was needed.

Dear Martha. So lonely without you tonight. Don't know if I can last this trip out. Love, Harold.

Well! So Martha had a lover named Harold. Good for Martha. Keep track. Must find out how lovers are getting on.

Dearest. So sorry to hear you are sick. Get the best doctor. Love, Harold.

So Martha is sick, is she? How unfortunate. It is bad enough for lovers to be separated, without adding sickness. Maybe Martha gets a mysterious wire without any signature.

Don't you worry, Martha. Everything will be all right. I know. You just keep faith.

Dear Harold. Just received strangest wire. Who could have sent it? Love, Martha.

Up in his tiny cubicle, the old man was back among the living. He was a robot no longer.

"I tell you, he *does* send telegrams," Slats insisted. "I've seen them. Sometimes he sends five or six a week. That's the only damned thing that's good about this Depression. People are fighting to stay human. When the Depression ends, everybody will change, including me. The cities will get bigger, and worse, and then . . ."

"Then what?"

Slat's voice trailed off. If he knew, he wasn't telling. He reflected for a long time, then his mood abruptly changed.

"That's the way it is. And it's sad to think that it's all gonna change. When it does, I'm gonna change with it. I'm gonna get mine. God, how did we get on this morbid subject?"

"We were talking about cities."

"Yeah. Well, that's what a city is. That's all I was saying."

A Trace of Weird

There was something about the house that compelled him: three stories tall, with twin spires, it looked like a Hollywood adaptation of Charles Addams. The shingles were bleached gray. Tiny windows in the spires looked like gun ports in a Spanish galleon. All right, he said. A perfect sanctuary where he could hide for a while, add things up, where he could lick his wounds when he got fired from his latest job—which he was sure would happen soon.

A tall pine tree standing like a lonely sentinel in the front yard had something to do with his decision: It dwarfed the scrub palms on the block; the fact that the tree was dead did not occur to him.

He went to the front door and pushed the bell. It opened almost at once, slowly, cautiously, revealing an obese, elderly woman.

"I'm sorry," Keltnor said, at the same time castigating himself for having apologized. After all, there *was* a "Room for Rent" sign in the window. Behind her, he saw the figure of an old man standing in what seemed a crooked, unnatural position, until he noticed the large hump on the man's back.

"Saw your sign. You have a room for rent?"

"Eight dollars the week. Payment in advance." She spoke in a flat, nasal voice that had the Midwest in it. "No guests in the room. No radio after ten o'clock. We are quiet people. This is my husband."

The humpbacked man gave a little tremor of greeting, consisting mostly of a wiggling of fingers of the right hand.

"Could I see the room?" Keltnor asked, wondering what force, what power, compelled him to remain standing there.

"You will see it when I take you there. No drinking. No noise. We're quiet people. There is a rocking chair on the front porch."

"I see it."

"For visitors."

"What?"

"If you have visitors, use the porch,"

Keltnor felt a commingling of strange emotions creep over him: horror of a kind, revulsion certainly, and anger. So why did he not flee? Why stand there, rooted to the spot, staring at this strange couple? "I'll take it," he said, as he watched himself pay out the eight dollars and follow the woman upstairs.

The room was just that—a room: a dresser and a rush mat that filled a square between the dresser, the cot, and the tiny windows. Another cot stood on the far side of the room—for double occupancy, Keltnor decided, if business got better. That was not likely to happen; rooms for rent were a glut on this market. Every block had several signs in the windows.

"I hope you enjoy your stay with us," said the old woman tonelessly. She closed the door.

Keltnor looked at himself in the mirror: You are positively an idiot to stay here, he told himself. Your brains must be taking a permanent vacation.

Could be, he mused. Life for him, during this period, was full of inconsistencies, if not downright irrationality. It was a time in his life when he was trying for *respectability*,

California style. He had a cubicle in a newspaper building, and a telephone. He was selling classified advertising. He had already, during this phase, tried a variety of forms of door-to-door selling: vacuum cleaners, aluminum ware, baby pictures, cosmetics. If one took the Los Angeles want ads seriously, there was no Depression at all. Hundreds of daily ads screamed and pleaded to those who could "sell." No experience needed. "If you believe in yourself, you can sell our product." As simple as that.

Keltnor wasn't sure he believed in himself. Come right down to it, he found that he could believe more in the products than he could in himself. They were so shiny. The selling propositions were so convincing. Each one was more intriguing, more amusing, than the other. How anyone could fail to become successful and affluent was beyond him. But not quite. After only a few experiences, he knew that it was all a kind of dream. As dreamlike and unreal as Hollywood itself. In short, synonymous with Hollywood, for all the dream-chasers in America seemed to have converged there. The quality of life seemed to be the focal point, a synthesis of the very essence of the American experience. How could anyone resist it? Certainly not Keltnor, and he readily succumbed.

During this phase, Keltnor came to have a dim awareness, as he walked the Hollywood streets at night, that all he really had at this point in this life was his youth. And during the darker moments of his spirit, this hardly seemed enough.

After a week, Keltnor ardently reconfirmed his earlier conclusion: He was an idiot to stay here. Yet he stayed. The house, its mood, and the silence began to affect him in strange ways. For one thing, he had never thought about the quality, the essence, of silence. Here, it was thick, stifling. Not a sound could be heard from the man and woman downstairs. He found himself tiptoeing across the third floor room, as though fearful of the consequences should he make a noise. Even the sound of the boards in the floor made him self-conscious. Any unexpected, self-induced sound, like urinating directly into the toilet bowl, instead of along the sides, startled him, because he knew they would hear it. But the muffled sounds of the outside world came through, and they were intolerable because they were so intrusive. From a nearby schoolyard, he could hear the sounds of children at play. The bells of a nearby church—it had to be Catholic, so obsessed was it with the sound of its bells—intruded often. Each time they tolled, they had a different sound. In the morning they were harsh, demanding: Get up! Get out! Do something! At noon, the bells varied. Sometimes they were pleasing; other times, rasping. In the late afternoon, they rang the Angelus, which was the worst of all: dolorous, baleful, agonizing. It was even worse than the funeral dirge thantolled occasionally in the mornings.

By then, Keltnor had gotten himself fired from the newspaper. Not because he could not sell classified ads. He rather enjoyed telling lies over the telephone to people who wanted to hear them. As long as he knew they wanted to hear his lies, it was alright. And fun. He knew it couldn't go on forever; he had no intention of continuing at this career very long, but he got himself fired sooner than he would have otherwise, simply because he wanted to do some thinking.

Or was it the house?

For a brief period there was a welcome intrusion in the form of a second roomer. Keltnor resented him at first. But he was so pleasant, so amiable, that Keltnor knew he wouldn't stay in the house very long. Therefore, Keltnor didn't mind.

The new roomer was tall, Italian, Catholic, and reasonably well educated. He had been sent out by his parents, who apparently could afford it, on a safari to "crash the pictures." He had good books and a constant smile. His name was Nino and he did not really care whether he achieved success in pictures or not. As far as Keltnor was concerned, this was another reason for forgiving him the instrusion.

Nino sat around every day at the casting offices of the studios. "The way you do it," he said, "is you make a pest of yourself. Like a sit-down strike. Sooner or later they notice you."

Occasionally, they did notice Nino. He had carried a spear in a costume picture recently, and since he had established a "credit" of having successfully carried one spear, he was on call to carry another spear in another costume picture. But the logistics went bad in his second picture. He hitchhiked or bussed out to Culver City every day for a week, only to find the scene postponed.

In the meantime, Nino came upon other adventures. His greatest (which Keltnor absolutely believed, because Nino was too young, too happy, to lie,) concerned an old lady ("at least eighty") who had picked Nino up in her electric car driving along Sunset Boulevard.

The story of what the old lady did to Nino with her toothless gums was wonderful and Keltnor felt that he had come back to life again. He found the story neither salacious nor offensive. After all, Nino had what the old woman needed—youth. And she had what Nino needed—money. He roared over the description, forgetting that his laughter would be heard throughout the house. For those few days that Nino was there, Keltnor completely forgot about the house.

Then Nino left. Quite suddenly. He simply disappeared one day while Keltnor was taking a walk.

With Nino gone, things got worse. Keltnor began to feel that he was being watched. Once, he stopped at the top of the hall stairs to tie his shoes, and a shiver ran down his spine. He had the positive feeling that someone was behind him. As he straightened up, he saw the humpbacked man watching him from the shadows. His head was curiously cocked; his small eyes expressionless.

Another time he caught the obscenely fat old woman watching him from an unnatural position. It was an instant only, a freeze in time; he could not account for the feeling of terror that riffled through him. She was standing there, doubled over, gazing at him through the crook of her arm; the other arm holding aside one of her breasts so that she could see. Then she moved again, reached down to pick up a ball of yarn. A faint smile struggled across her face.

"You are very quiet. That's good."

"Thank you," said Keltnor, and he tiptoed upstairs.

A week later or was it two, or a month?—time had lost its thread—Keltnor learned of the presence of another body in this living tomb. Keltnor's schedule had reversed by now: He was reading all night because the quality of silence was exquisite then—not even the outside world intruded—and he was sleeping most of the day. Late in the afternoon, he tiptoed out for breakfast. There he found sitting in the rocking chair on the porch an ancient emaciated, angular-faced woman staring transfixed at the sky. Her eyes were half-closed; at first, Keltnor though she was dead.

He shuddered, ate nothing that afternoon, and he walked the streets far into the night, thinking; asking himself, what was happening?

Several days later, when he again ran into the wife and had the courage to speak, he learned that the ancient woman was her mother.

"She can't walk. Once a week we carry her to the rocking chair and she sits."

"Oh." Perhaps I am going crazy, Keltnor told himself. Perhaps I have retreated as far as I can, to the very outer limits, and beyond that is the point of no return. Or is it this damned house?

Driven by curiosity to find out what it was like "downstairs" in the living tomb, Keltnor waited one day until they were gone. He watched them drive off in their vintage Essex, and decided that this was the time to find out. He had lost track of days by now and only knew that it was Sunday because a radio was blaring away in the neighborhood and the announcer was describing the antics of a professional football game.

Treading softly in his worn sneakers, Keltnor made his way down the stairs where the "secret" lay. Just where, precisely, he had no idea; but he was sure he would find it.

Where, he asked himself, does one look to find the secret of lives? The library, of course. Where the books were. If there were no books, that in itself would be an answer.

The stairs passed the entrance to the dining room, which he had glimpsed on occasion when the sliding door was left ajar. Entering it now, he found another door leading to the left. This led into a room that served as a library, for there were a few books on a shelf of one wall staring forlornly down at a museum of bric-a-brac: mementos, seashells, and souvenirs collected over half a century.

Keltnor seized a volume. But before he glanced at its title, he accustomed his eyes to the gloom and took inventory of the room. Thickly brocaded drapes shut out the sunshine. Vague shapes began to take form. A fireplace, blocked up. A hand-woven tapestry, so faded he could scarcely make out the outline of two cupids hovering over an unidentifiable object. Two fish bowls contained brightly colored stones—but otherwise empty. A bird cage, also empty; with several tiny yellow feathers lying on the bottom. The feed tray was partially full.

Keltnor looked at the volume he had picked up. The title startled him:

How to Be a Success.

Other volumes next to where it had been, read:

How to Make Money
How to Be Popular with Those You Love
How to Achieve Wealth and Happiness.

Keltnor searched for the publication dates of each of the volumes. All had been published before the turn of the century.

Then he found a tattered photo album. It began with tintypes of the husband and wife when they were infants. Faithfully, it plotted the various stages of their lives: childhood, adolescence, youth. Then, the critical juncture when their lives joined. "We Get Married," read the ornate, Palmer-style script; under it, a picture of their wedding, dated March 2, 1884.

Thereafter, a poignant trip through time. Their first home in Grand Island, Nebraska. Their farm in Kansas. Their three automobiles, including their present Essex, which had been purchased in 1925. Their vacations—not many: Niagara Falls. A Chautauqua in Colorado. Grand Canyon. Yosemite Falls. Their faces grew more blank with each passing year. As the quality of the photograph improved technically, their faces became more anonymous.

Keltnor's stomach grew queasy. In the space of a few minutes, he had gone through two lives. All of it! Nothing was missing. That's all there was. He felt faint.

Then, as if his horror were not complete, Keltnor turned and saw the old grandmother sitting in her rocking chair in the doorway. How long she had been there, he did not know.

"That's our picture album," she said.

Keltnor's blood ran cold. Mostly, because he could tell that she was *trying* to show emotion.

She was trying to smile.

As if this were not enough, the next day Keltnor was confronted by the wife at the bottom of the stairs.

"I understand you were looking at our picture album."

"Yes."

"We're just ordinary people, as you see. You are quiet. Well behaved. We like that. You must be lonely in your room."

For a reason Keltnor could not explain, he said yes.

"Why don't you come downstairs tonight and spend an evening with us?"

Again, to his chagrin, he agreed.

They sat in the same small vault of a den that evening; each of them in separate corners illuminated by the pale colors of a Tiffany lamp. The husband sat hunched forward, gazing down at the patterns in the rug, his hump sharply silhouetted; the grandmother rocked gently in her wheel-chair.

"We're just plain, simple people," they repeated. They had retired twenty years ago from their farm in Kansas. They had worked hard, struggled, saved frugally; now they were living out the rest of their days in "peace and quiet." The Depression did not bother them. They had never been creatures of "extravagance." "We do with very little. Our needs are simple. We do not complain."

They went through the picture album again.

When Keltnor could no longer stand it, when he felt a sense of suffocation, as though unseen hands were clutching at his throat, he arose, quietly said goodnight, and escaped to his room.

A few days later, Keltnor ran into Nino on Hollywood Boulevard. They went into Thrifty's Drug Store, where Nino treated him to a milkshake. Nino was doing well. He had carried a spear successfully in his second picture and had now been given a one-line speaking part in a Western.

"What's the line?" asked Keltnor.

Nino laughed. "I'm a Mexican. I shout, 'Caramba! Look out! Deesa gringo gotta gun!'"

Keltnor congratulated him. "I like Mexicans who speak with an Italian accent." After a moment, he looked at Nino. "Tell me," he asked, "why did you leave the room?"

"Too spooky. It started to get to me. Are you still there?"

Keltnor nodded. "But I'm leaving. Now I can leave."

"What do you mean, 'now'?"

Keltnor did not bother to explain. He wasn't sure Nino would understand.

A few days after that, Keltnor did leave. Why stay longer? he asked himself. He had learned the secret of the house and its people. It was time to get on now with the things that youths must do.

A year later, still on the move, Keltnor returned to Hollywood. He went back to the house on Curson Street to see how his "friends" were doing.

The house was empty. A For Sale sign was nailed to the tree.

All three members of the family, he learned from neighbors, had died. The tall, emaciated grandmother had rocked herself to death on the front porch one sunny afternoon, her eyes remaining open, fixed on the tall, dead pine tree. The wife had died six months later. She lingered in illness for several months and apparently grew angry at the fact that her husband would succeed her. She changed her will, renounced her husband and her distant relatives; everyone, in fact, except the Lord, Himself! She left everything to the temple of Aimee Semple McPherson.

The will was broken, of course, and her husband inherited his rightful goods, including the house and the Essex. He promptly hired a comely, middle-aged nurse and began preparing for a long vacation. But the poor fellow lost his balance one day and tumbled headlong down the steep stairs leading from the second floor. The nurse, having detected a stench from inside the house, found the hunchback's body. She quickly fled.

Keltnor felt sorry to hear the news, but not as sorry as he knew he should be. All he could bring himself to feel was a gentle sadness at the waste. Nature, he concluded, was prodigious in all things—including waste.

Once again, Keltnor tried to articulate the meaning of his experience there. Maybe, he told himself, man is born to suffer. And struggle. And love. Maybe if he misses any of these, he does not succeed at becoming whole. The Morgan family—for that was their name—probably had suffered.

Certainly they had struggled. But maybe love was something they had never had; neither the receiving of it, nor the giving of it. And yet, surely, they would have denied this.

Now, a year later, the answer did not concern him as much as it had a year before. There was too much else to do. A trace of weird, Keltnor told himself, and he let it go at that. The time for adding it all up, making sense of it—that time would come later.

Solid Citizen

Next to his job, Ollie Ward guessed he loved his town more than anything else. Like most towns in Iowa, the town of Affinity prided itself on being the "friendliest, most progressive" town in the entire state. With only eighteen hundred people, it boasted of two stoplights, one at each end of Main Street. "We don't need them now, but we're building for the future," said the mayor.

Affinity had a new Reo fire truck, a band of forty—with five gleaming tubas, a well-kept fairground and baseball diamond, an aggressive Farmers Co-op, and the *Affinity Beacon*, a weekly paper that prided itself on its bold, stand-up-for-justice editorials. It came out strongly in favor of the practice of dumping milk on the highways to bolster the sagging price of milk, and for the prevention of farm foreclosures by self-styled "protective vigilantes." When "money greed" mortgage agents attempted to foreclose on certain farms in the country, the *Beacon* editorialized: "It's fortunate that no one has been killed so far, but let us not become complacent. The foreclosures are going on all over the state and continued attempts can be expected in this area. We suggest that an empty gun is of absolutely no value. An empty gun is an empty bluff. Those who come with empty shotguns are not doing their part."

Ollie thought this was about as courageous a way of "laying it on the line" as he had ever seen. He personally visited Henry Moore, the editor and publisher, and told him how proud he was to see the Higby Department Store shoe ads appear on the same pages with the editorial. "As manager of the shoe department, I just had to tell you this," said Ollie. "I have also conveyed my feelings on the matter to Mr. Higby."

Henry Moore thanked him and suggested that the proper way for Jasper Higby to show his appreciation was to buy more advertising space.

Ollie had many good points and very few faults. He was incessantly cheerful, always bubbling with good spirits. He was a bachelor, nearing thirty, and he lived with and supported his mother. He led a clean life and seldom drank. His face was slightly florid and his weight reflected a tendency toward too much apple pie and corn on the cob. He had no real vices unless one considered as a vice his ineffable optimism and a tendency to exaggerate the truth. Many considered him to be Affinity's greatest booster. Knockers had no place in Ollie's scheme of things. To him, Affinity was the finest town in the finest state in the finest country in the world, not only now, but in the past and future as well.

To top all of this off, Ollie had a job that he considered the most thrilling occupation one could have. To tenderly massage a pretty young girl's feet was a treat that never failed to send chills of pleasure up and down his spine. His greatest thrill came from young, newly married women and young boys.

His prowess at massaging feet became a subject of conversation in some circles, particularly among the ladies, but he did not mind. To make sure that no one could gossip or accuse him of showing partiality, he made a point of rubbing *all* feet, including those of weather-beaten, taciturn farmers and old ladies. He would give them a brisk rub with both hands, and the stern admonition: "Protect your feet no matter what. They are your most important possession. Let them go, and your health goes. Let your arches fall, and your posture changes. It affects your spine, then you're in deep trouble."

But with the young women of town it was a different story. Reactions varied:

"Oh, that Ollie Ward. He is really something when he takes your foot in his hands. I get tingly all over."

"Not me. I feel creepy inside. The way he goes around it, I mean. He half-closes his eyes and seems to be off in another world."

"Well, you've got to admit, it's something different. His hands are so soft. If I asked my husband to do that, the calluses would hurt."

With the young bachelors of Affinity, to hear Ollie tell it, his conquests and adventures were legion. He was always running off to Chicago or some place on weekends. When he returned, he sat with the boys on the sidewalk in from of Quackenbush's Drug Store, sharing his tales of salacious delights which, even if not true, were worth the listening.

"I was in Chicago last weekend. What a broad I met! She invited me to her apartment. Her girlfriend was there. We all got drunk. And, what those two did to each other . . ."

"To each other?" Eyes would pop.

"Of course! Haven't you heard about that?"

"To hell with *that*. What did they do to you?"

"You can't imagine. But relax. I'll give you the hot scoop . . ."

And torrid it was. By the time Ollie finished, the men were decidedly uncomfortable, wondering privately if they still had their hidden copies of *Paris Nights, Police Gazatte, or Captain Billy's Whizbang.*

The fact of the matter is, Ollie Wash had not gone to Chicago that weekend, or any other weekend. He had gone to Davenport, eighty miles away, where he always went on weekends. There, he had checked into the Blackhawk Hotel, Room 418, which he always asked for because it had an unusually large and clear mirror facing the bed. Then, retracing his steps, he went back to the bus station to pick up a special suitcase which he always kept in a certain locker.

As he approached the locker, he inadvertently bumped into a stranger. The stranger happened to be Keltnor, who was there for the purpose of cleaning himself up after an overnight freight ride from Chicago. He had gotten off at the Silvis freight yards, and now, in the bus station, was debating whether to get out of Davenport on freights or hitchhike across the state. First, he wanted to get the "straight dope" on whether Iowa was hospitable to hitch-hikers, as he had heard.

Keltnor's glance, after the slight collision, and a mumbled "'scuse me," revealed an assured, smiling, slightly corpulent, medium-sized man, and it gave Keltnor a flash of envy: Here, in the midst of the Depression, was a fellow who, obviously from his appearance, had already found his place. He *fit* somewhere, which, after all, was the important thing. He lived in a state that typified all of the solid virtues: hard work, responsibility, no nonsense about life. Here were people who were reliable, trustworthy, decent, as American as apple pie, and who, despite the Depression, lived on soil that was richer, more productive per square foot than any in the country. Which was why Iowans were so secure, so proud: No one could take their soil away from them. How nice it would be some day, Keltnor reflected, if he could fit somewhere, someplace.

Ollie's good spirits, which always erupted at the unexpected and were mainly a nervous reflex, made Keltnor smile. Then the moment was over. Ollie watched the stranger disappear; he looked around, surveyed the scene to be sure no one was watching him, and finally he opened the locker. He took from it an inexpensive suitcase and returned to Room 418 at the Blackhawk. There, he opened it and carefully laid the contents out on the bed. They consisted of a complete female wardrobe. Nothing was missing: sheer black hose, spike-heeled shoes, panties, padded bra, three different dresses, a wig, and a makeup kit.

Ollie took off his clothes and slowly dressed before the mirror, reveling in the transformation. From an ordinary, plain male, he was turning into an alluring, sexual woman. At last it came time for the most fun of all: putting on the makeup. Heavy mascara, scented rouge, scarlet lipstick, Chanel perfume. The thrill was always a new one. He stood there startled and overwhelmed by the vision of God's handiwork that revealed itself in the mirror. He set in place a few curls of the long blond wig, touched his provocative breasts, and examined his shapely legs sheathed in sheer black hose. Finally, Ollie pronounced himself "ready."

He went to the door, stealthily opened it, and whispered: "Okay, Arnold. You can come in now."

Closing the door, Ollie smiled seductively at his friend: "I thought you'd never come. What took you so long? Now Arnold, please. Not yet. Keep your hands to yourself. I'll tell you when."

The truth, of course, was that there was no one in the room. But Ollie never thought of it this way. To him, Arnold (last name, Greyson) was a friend of long standing, and he was unquestionably there. In fact, it had been in this very room, 418, that they had first met three years ago. Ever since then, they had been inseparable. However, only here in Davenport did they dare to do anything intimate. Back in Affinity, they simply went on long walks out near the fairground and exchanged ideas on life and "what it's all about." But here, on Saturdays, they could do the most thrilling things together. Absolutely delicious, incredible, unbelievable things!

"How do you like it, Arnold?" Ollie asked as he paraded before the mirror studying himself, yet keeping a wary eye on Arnold who was sitting on the bed.

"Do you like what you see?"

"Of course," replied Arnold.

"Does it do things to you?"

"Plenty," said Arnold.

"Tell me—what does it do to you? Arnold—wait! Not yet. Remember what I said. We must do it my way. You promised the last time."

"I know, but . . ." Arnold seemed terribly tense.

"Please, Arnold. Keep your zipper up. Remember the promise we made last week? Remember the awful quarrel we had? Let's not have another one." Ollie assumed an alluring, faintly lascivious pose before the mirror: one hand on hip, the other pulling up the skirt to reveal delectable thighs. "Do you like that, Arnold?"

"I sure do."

"Would you like me to take something off?"

"Of course. What are we waiting for?"

"All right. If you promise to be a good boy and not to touch. Remember, you *mustn't* touch until I give the word."

Slowly, tantalizingly, Ollie began to disrobe. The dress slipped daintily over the blond head, scarcely upsetting a curl. He could tell what a difficult time Arnold was having in trying to control himself. Arnold was clutching himself in exquisite agony. His zipper was open. How cute, thought Ollie. How like a man. Ollie flicked his tongue out over his full, luscious red lips. "Arnold, you bad boy. You said you'd wait. What are you doing?

"To hell with waiting," said Arnold

"Well, I guess I can't blame you, naughty boy. If what you see gives you so much pleasure, how can I deny you?" Ollie caressed himself wantonly, his own breathing heavy. He told himself, not yet—a little longer.

"Oh Arnold, you *do* like it, don't you? How wondrous are the workings of the Lord. Think of it! It all fits into His scheme of things. I like it, too. So very much! And, to tell the truth, I can't stand this torture much longer . . ."

Suddenly, Ollie threw himself on the bed in a kind of frenzy. He began undulating wildly. "Oh yes, Arnold. Now! Do it now! Quickly, Arnold! I can't wait another second. Please, Arnold, yes, anything, just do it, oh Lord, oh Bless the Lord for all His wonders . . ."

A few minutes later, Ollie was sound asleep, one of those blissful, deep, exhausted, dreamless sleeps that bless only innocent children or the very old. He slept for nearly twelve hours. It was the middle of the night when he awoke. He read his Gideon Bible for a while, then fell off again.

The next morning, Ollie went to church, and afterward, took a long, leisurely walk along a street that paralleled the Mississippi. Later, he went to a movie house and saw *Lives of a Bengal Lancer*, staring Gary Cooper.

It was not until late that night that Ollie arrived home.

He took the last bus back to Affinity, and instructed the driver to let him off at the edge of town. From there, he walked along a sycamore-lined side street that led to his mother's home.

Mondays after weekends in Davenport were always Ollie's best day. He felt refreshed, invigorated, replenished. He scarcely could wait until the day was over to sit in the evening with the fellows at Quackenbush's, on chairs in front of the store if the weather was nice, or inside if it was cold.

The talk that summer Monday night was desultory. The vibrations were not strong in any direction. Nobody had anything to complain about or brag about. No one was particularly angry at life or pleased with it. There was the usual mild argument about the Hit Parade. The new number one hit song was "All My Eggs in One Basket," replacing "Chapel in the Moonlight." Several of the fellows favored "Pennies from Heaven" and "Moon over Miami," but they did so without any particular passion. On Saturday night, a human fly had scaled the tallest building in town, the four-story Schroeder Hotel, with its flat, red brick façade, so smooth and slick that it defied any honest human scaling. Doc Hilliard, the new young bachelor dentist in Affinity, insisted that the "human fly" was a fraud, that the building could not be scaled without "devices."

"He must have had talons, or some sort of device, to penetrate the mortar between the bricks," said Doc. "I'm personally convinced of that. Otherwise, it couldn't be done."

Red Barn, the roadhouse three miles outside of town, had been relatively quiet over the weekend, reported Al Finch, the town's plumber. Only one fight between two farmers over a woman, and that was all. Not a single person had been thrown into Affinity's jail over the weekend. Things had been dull indeed.

Ollie waited patiently for his opening. Then, with a hearty chuckle, to warn that something important was coming, he announced, "Well, I had some action over the weekend, let me tell you that boys. It was fantastic!"

"Really, Ollie? Where did you go?"

Ollie shrugged. "Chicago."

"Again?"

"Yeah, I shouldn't go there so often, I know. I'm overdue to go back to Minneapolis—I've got something lovely stashed there. It's just that . . . there are so many things going on in Chicago. And last Saturday was too much."

Phil Archer, son of Asher Archer, Affinity's mortician, coughed rather ominously.

"Really, Ollie? Tell us about it."

"Well, I tell you boys, I thought I'd seen everything till last weekend. This was too much."

Emil Schultz, the high school math teacher, snorted skeptically: "What was it this time, Ollie? Two girls and a dog?" The others laughed.

"Wait a minute," said Ollie. "Listen to this. You fellows ever hear of a place called Stickney?" No one had ever heard of Stickney. "It's a little suburb outside of Chicago. Al Capone runs it."

"You met Al there, I suppose. I'll bet you're both good friends by now."

"Hold on. Nothing like that. This is the real McCoy, what I'm going to tell you. Like I just said, Capone's outfit runs that place in Stickney. You know what kind of establishment I'm talking about, don't you?"

"A ladies tea shop."

Ollie roared. "Very good, Emil. I'll have to remember that. Anyhow . . ." And so Ollie launched into his story about the whorehouse in Stickney where he not only had witnessed but had been participant in a "show" that did, indeed, include two girls, one dog, and a "fairy."

When he finished, the rest, if not enthralled, did seem to be properly impressed.

"I sure would like to have seen that," said Bix Fletcher, a mechanic.

"Hey, hotshot," said Al Finch, "why don't you take me with you on one of those trips?"

Then, out of nowhere, Phil Archer dropped his bomb. "He couldn't take you with him to Chicago, Al, because he doesn't go to Chicago on weekends."

"What do you mean, Phil?" Ollie asked.

"You weren't in Chicago last weekend," said Phil, staring straight at Ollie.

"I don't understand . . ."

"I'll tell you what you are, Ollie Ward. You're a liar!"

Ollie winced. "Phil, I don't understand."

"You understand all right."

Phil obviously knew something and was biding his time, baiting Ollie, and letting him fall into his trap. The others remained silent, watching Ollie carefully. Ollie used the time as best he could to decide how to proceed. A calm, reasonable approach, he decided, would be the best.

"Phil, I don't get what you're driving at. *Of course*, I was in Chicago. I was in a whorehouse in Stickney, just like I told you."

"No, you weren't. You were in Davenport."

"Davenport?" Ollie appeared confused. "Why would I

be in Davenport, when I was in Chicago?"

"I don't know why. But that's where you were, because I saw you there."

"Saw *me*?"

"Yes. Saw *you*."

"How could you see me, when I was in Chicago?"

"You were walking along River Street about noon, on Sunday, and I was driving by—I was visiting my uncle there—and I saw you just as plain as the nose on my face."

"It couldn't have been me. It must be a case of mistaken identify."

"No sir. You turned your face as I passed. You didn't see me, but I saw you. I wasn't twenty feet away. I said to myself, 'That's Ollie Ward. What's he doing here?' I was going to yell at you, but by that time I had passed, and there was traffic. I had to watch where I was going. So I said to myself, well, I'll find out Monday what Ollie was doing in Davenport."

Doc Hilliard chimed in. "C'mon, Ollie, if it's the truth, admit it. There's no crime in being in Davenport on Sunday."

Al Finch laughed: "No crime, but not much fun, either."

Ollie felt himself hemmed in. All he could do was plead: "C'mon, Phil, you're not being fair . . ."

"Fair? You're not being truthful. You're a damned liar, that's what you are, Ollie Ward. I wouldn't believe you on a stack a Bibles."

"Please, Phil . . ."

"You and the truth are total strangers. To put it mildly, you've got an overworked imagination. I don't think you can recognize the truth when you see it. Like the time you told my kid brother you'd been offered a job on an expedition to India. Indiana might have been more like it."

Phil scored heavily with this thrust. The raucous laughter made Ollie feel like he was on fire.

"You told someone you were going out with Mary Cassidy, and that she offered to go all the way with you the very first time. I happen to know Mary Cassidy never *once* went out with you."

"But she did, Phil . . ."

"Like hell she did. Closest you ever got to Mary Cassidy was her feet! And what you did to her feet, she said, gave her the creeps."

Every man has his vulnerable point and Ollie's had been struck. The fellows roared. Bix Fletcher stuck out his foot; "Hey, Ollie, how about giving me a massage? The works." Five solid young citizens of Affinity, Iowa, collapsed in laughter. Each one took off a shoe and extended a foot. The howls of glee rang through the semi-deserted streets. Ollie staggered to his feet. There was nothing to do but retreat. But why this sudden hostility? Why were they all against him?

Phil wouldn't let up. "And that great genius friend of yours you're always talking about. That guy, Arnold Greyson. When's he coming to town so we can meet him?

Ollie literally stumbled out of their midst and around the corner where he leaned against the building stunned beyond belief. *How cruel one's fellow man can be!* He could still hear their laughter. and their voices.

"Poor Ollie! You were too hard on him, Phil."

"Yeah, Phil, what got into you?"

"I don't know," said Phil. "Sometimes he gets on my nerves, with all his lies. . . ."

"But that's just his way, Phil. Ollie will never change.

You have to accept him as he is. After all, he means well."

"Sure. We all have our faults. At heart, old Ollie's a good enough guy. He's got his place at Higby's. He takes good care of his mother . . ."

"I guess you're right," said Phil.

There was a reflective pause, as though all of them were regretful at being so rough on Ollie. Doc Hilliard, the dentist, summed it up: "Ollie may lay it on a little thick now and then, but that's just his way. If you ask me, I predict that one day he'll end up being one of our most solid citizens. A guy that this town can be really proud of. Affinity could use more guys like Ollie Ward."

Ollie stood there, overwhelmed now with pride, as he had been a moment before with shame. So, they *didn't* really dislike him! He *belonged*! He was one of them! "A solid citizen!" Think of it, he told himself. The responsibility. The challenge of those words made him feel older, more mature. And happier than he could ever remember having been . He heard Emil Schultz say, "Well it's almost 'Amos 'n' Andy' time. I'm goin' home guys."

Ollie tiptoed away from the building and walked rapidly down the street to the edge of town, to the fairgrounds. The moon was heavy in the sky, and bright. It cast long, deep shadows over the grandstand and along the baseball diamond. He looked at it all and felt as though he would burst with pride. His beloved town of Affinity, where he now truly belonged. And to think that he had been harboring certain furtive dreams about leaving it—going to the city, some other town, uprooting himself. What would he be but just another alienated soul who belonged nowhere? Now, he told himself, he could truly settle down.

Out of the shadows stepped his friend, Arnold Greyson.

Arnold's appearance did not surprise him. Well, tonight was as good a time as any to break it off, once and for all.

"Hello, Ollie! How goes it tonight?"

"Just fair," said Ollie. "What's on your mind?"

"Is that the way to greet me? What's wrong?"

"As a matter of fact, Arnold, I'm glad you came tonight. We have something to talk about."

"Like what?"

"To put it bluntly, it's all over between us. I'm sorry, but that's the way it's got to be."

"What do you mean?"

"I can't see you anymore."

"Why not?"

"I can't, that's all."

Arnold seemed angry. "That's a hell of a thing to say, after all we've been through."

"I know it. And I'm sorry. But that's the way it's got to be. I've come to a turning point in my life."

"I think I'm owed some kind of explanation."

"I can't, Arnold. I simply can't. Now don't go making it hard for me. Let's just call it quits, right here and now."

Arnold was deeply offended. "Hell, if that's the way you feel about it, okay. Some day you may need me and I won't be around. But that's all right. I've got other friends. I don't exactly need you for happiness in this life. It's a big ocean and there's a lot of fish in it. Good-bye." And with that, Arnold Greyson headed in the direction of the shadows of the grandstand.

Ollie watched him depart. Other than a slight tinge of regret, he felt no strong emotions. If he was going to be a solid citizen, it meant good-bye to a lot of things in his life. No more weekends in Davenport, that much was for sure.

Good-bye to Room 418. But still, he had his career. He still would be selling shoes and massaging feet. Thank God that wouldn't be taken away from him.

But his bachelorhood, he realized, would also have to end. Despite the fact that he never had any strong desire to marry, now he would have to take a wife. One could not be a solid citizen of Affinity without being married. And after that, there would be children. All of these things would have to come about—and soon—if he was truly going to become a solid citizen.

But they were worth it, he mused. Yes, he had no doubts.

As he scuffed along the outfield of the baseball diamond, a solitary figure in the gray moonlight, his mind began ticking off possible marriage prospects. He felt much older. And a little regretful that the past, which had been so much fun, was over. Yet he also felt a deep pride in what the future would bring. He was now a solid citizen.

Travelers

Max Baer was fighting that night, which was a sufficient link with reality for Keltnor to know just where he was on his own special route to eternity: midmorning on a late summer day in 1939. The rest of his link was nature itself. Highway 10 winding its way to Seattle from Coeur d'Alene, Spokane, and Moses Lake. Pine trees standing proud, looking down from every side. A clean blue sky; air so pure it seemed a shame to filter it through his city-contaminated lungs.

Damned if he hadn't been traveling some these past six years, Keltnor mused. Snooping around, looking at America. Some kind of country, too, not caring if there was a Depression beginning or ending. The land just lays there, he thought, kind of aloof, not caring. The land really owns us, not the other way around. I hope it stays that way, he told himself.

He thought of some of the places he'd been: Ketchum, Kimberly, and Kooskin. Red Bud, Rosebud, Red Blood, Bad Blood. Galena and Goliath, but not Goochland, Halifax, Solomon, or Grundy. Pekin, Moscow, Paris, Dublin, and New London. But not Rome, Algiers, or Canton. Apalachicola and Chattahoochee. But not Kissimmee, Wemehitchka, or Punta Gorda. Owasso, Paw Paw, and Petoskey. Mesquits, Midas, and Nixon. Tungsten. But not Weed Heights or Paradise Valley. Sounds like poetry, Keltnor laughed. Makes no sense, but it's fun to say the words out loud.

Seattle—48 miles

Only two places on the map that he still wanted to see: What Cheer, and Lost Nation, Iowa. Towns with names like that couldn't be all bad. Especially, Lost Nation. What Cheer, also, if the founding burghers had thought to put a question mark after the name What Cheer? But, Lost Nation, now that name *said* something. Exquisite symbolism: Here we are, folks, a lost nation, hiding in the cornfield. If my name were Rand or McNally, he thought, I'd print on every map:

United States of America
Home of Lost Nation

How come Rand doesn't tell McNally that? Or somebody tell Rand? Maybe I'll write him a letter.

Walking along the road, too contented even to extend his hitchhiking thumb, Keltnor came to the top of a rise. There stood a log cabin restaurant. Modern service trying to hide its face, nestling in the pines, off the road, looking storybook pretty. A solitary car was gleaming in the sunshine. New LaSalle four-door, Alabama license plates. Deep South, he thought, you're a long ways from home. He fantasized about some middle-aged, respectable, middle-class family in vacation, enjoying the fruits of democracy, capitalism, U.S. highways, and Ford Motors. Correct that: General Motors made LaSalle. Anyhow, there they were, inside, happily eating, writing postcards, telling the folks back home how great the air was in the Pacific Northwest. Probably had some kids. "Hey Dad, will we see any Eskimos or trappers from Alaska in Seattle?"

Was this great, or not? You bet it was. It truly gave him a wrench. Some day *he* would be that happy family inside, with a shiny new car parked in front, his family enjoying the American Dream.

I will come back some day. And I'll sit in that same damned restaurant—if it's still there. Instead of hiking through the white alkaline dust of Idaho, I'll drive through it with the radio on, and I'll be humming along with the music, thinking how great it all was back in this time of my life.

So, he asked himself, what if he was fantasizing? Dreams were just as important as reality. Better, in some ways. And the dream just now was to tell his future family how it felt to tramp around this country in hot sneakers; the good and the bad, but especially, the good: How awfully damn good it felt to be young and alive!

Moments, he thought. So many wondrous, indescribable moments. Take a century to add them all up. Like the one he'd had a few days ago. Walking along a road in Oregon. That long, tall iron picket fence running along the highway, out in the middle of nowhere. Behind those bars, a real live honest-to-God funny farm. Or, as the movies would call it, a horror-packed insane asylum! With people clinging to the bars of the fence, shrieking and laughing, scratching themselves, waving their arms and uttering gibberish in a way that rattled the bones of his soul. Their cries had followed him for a mile or so, a memory that he knew would stay with him forever. Why did he feel that this, somehow, was a spiritual experience?

Before he passed out of earshot of the asylum, he thought of his friend the Letter Writer back in Chicago. He had always defended the Letter Writer among their cronies because the two of them had something in common. But it was a secret that even the Letter Writer did not know. Keltnor, too, liked to write his thoughts on paper. Not often. Only when the mood struck hard—right in the middle of his emotional solar plexus. For that purpose, he always carried a blank sheet of paper and a stub of pencil.

Now he pulled out that sheet of paper and pencil. Nearby was a large stone boulder. He sat down and began to write. The maniacal sounds from the insane asylum seemed appropriate . . . the proper leitmotiv . . . mood music for the soul . . .

The next day, the day after the Max Baer fight, Keltnor was in Seattle, wondering where to go next. Eugene, Oregon, seemed like a good bet. Maybe back down the coast, straight through Big Sur country, all the way to La Jolla, San Diego, and Tijuana.

Until he heard Hitler had invaded Poland.

September 2, 1939.

The sound of the Führer's gravely voice, beside itself with frenzy and rage, coming through the radio in the lobby of the Seattle YMCA. It scared the shit out of him.

Suddenly, he knew it was over. All of it. All busted. Through. *Finite.* The whole thing.

The Depression.

The Thirties.

The Decade.

The Era.

If a war did not signify the end of an era, what did?

Yes, that's the end of it, thought Keltnor. Waiting five years for the Depression to end, for things to settle down. Could have anchored myself a year ago. Jobs beginning to be more plentiful now. Glad I didn't take one. Five years of scrounging around; now, how many years of war? How many years after that to get settled down? We'll be the longest "waitin'-around" generation ever. So, laugh it off, Keltnor. Laugh *with* it. Laugh *at* it. Scratch the balls inside your soul and take it. Oh, Mother of Pandas in the mountains of China, help me keep a sense of humor. Plain, old-fashioned, psychotic, symbiotic laughter, best prescription for this patient.

So now he knew he had to go back. Go back and wait for the war to come. Spend some happy times with Tommy Touhy, the Dombrowski brothers, the Genesyk girls, the Letter Writer, and the others.

This is what Keltnor did after Hitler invaded Poland. He went home to wait for the war to happen in America.

The faces were gray and taut with suspicion as they huddled under the streetlamp on that corner in the Mexican district of Los Angeles. Strangers, they averted one another's glances, but kept an eye on the door marked Travel Bureau. Waiting, some of them for hours, for word of their fate. And their money, which they had already paid.

The ad in the classified section of the L.A. *Times* read: "Traveling to Chicago? Go with us and share the expense. Only eighteen dollars. Must travel light. Call Humbolt 3648." Another, advertising as the East-West Travel Bureau, boasted: "Cheapest transportation to Chicago." The phone number was the same.

When Keltnor called, a voice said, "Be at the corner of Lilac and Figuero tonight at nine o'clock."

Outside, at nine-o'clock, under the pale gloom of the milk-glass streetlamp, everyone waited. Smoking. Coughing.

Suspicious of each other. A Mexican took their money. Keltnor heard him mutter to an associate that business was so good tonight they would have to send out two cars. A few minutes later, the Mexican called to them from the doorway of the small frame hut.

"Everyone inside."

No one moved. They didn't trust "inside." Besides, there was a stench coming from inside. The Mexican grew angry. He had made this request three times.

"Please," he said. "They're cracking down on wildcatters. You don't wanna make trouble, no? You wanna get there, no? Then step inside, yes?"

"When is the bus coming?" a woman asked.

"What bus, lady?"

"The bus you advertised."

The Mexican sighed. "Travel, yes. Bus, no. We drive private cars to Chicago for eighteen dollar a head. Don't worry—we get you there."

"Your ad said 'bus,'" the woman persisted.

The way the Mexican smiled reminded Keltnor of Peter Lorre. "Read it again, lady. It says 'transportation.'"

"I want my money back," the woman demanded.

The door slammed. Then reopened. Peter Lorre stuck his head out, comically, trying to look apologetic and not succeeding. "No refunds, lady. We already ordered the cars. Soon they be here. They come, you get in, pronto! And off you go." He spat expertly into the dirt, pulled his head back, and slammed the door.

What the hell, thought Keltnor. A new experience. This should be fun. Cigarette smoke curled upward into the fog and haze which enshrouded them. *As long as I don't get stuck next to that nervous female.* He counted eight men and six women. How could fourteen people be crammed into two cars? Sensing that it would be something of a free-for-all for the best seats when the cars came, Keltnor edged toward the curb and kept an eye out for anything on wheels. When the cars came, he would give them a lesson in agility.

A moment later, as if on cue, a car rolled up and out stepped a tall, thin fellow wearing a huge sombrero. He disappeared into the waiting room of the "Travel Bureau."

Keltnor had no idea how it happened—except that he started it—but a moment later, seven people had crammed themselves into the car, which was a limousine of considerable vintage. *My God, it can't be true, but it is*, he thought: two in the front, five in the rear (one of them, a teenager, content sitting on the floor). Keltnor thought about the absurdity of it all.

A minute later the car door slammed and a voice said laconically, "All set? Let's go." The starter whined and the low-pitched engine sputtered to life. "My name is Slim. Give me no trouble, I give you none. We're going to Chicago. Straight through, if we can. Three days, three nights. No stopping except for gas, eats, and nature calls. If we get stopped by the police, remember, we're just friends driving east. Nobody paid money for no ride, understand? Wildcatting is against the law. You'll be put in jail and fined if you tell anyone you paid money for this trip. That's why nobody gave you a receipt. Okay? Let's go. It's a big country and we're gonna see some of it."

With that, the car moved forward, and Slim slouched over the wheel in a weary, relaxed manner, seemingly as bored as the rest were excited, fearful, and resentful.

Keltnor felt that this was as good a way as any to end a decade.

In the street-smart way Keltnor had developed over recent years, he decided to let the sorting out process happen *to him*, and not create it by conversation. They were a motley group, that was for sure. Hostile with each other and with the world. He couldn't blame them for being resentful. Solid, God-fearing, taxpaying citizens—once again they had been "taken" by American advertising. Here they were, packed in an old limousine headed for Chicago, and there was nothing they could do about it. Yet for eighteen dollars, what could they have expected? What Americans always expect—that bargain of bargains, that super bargain that never exists.

A young couple sat next to him, and from their conversation Keltnor judged them to be newlyweds. The bride chattered incessantly. From her talk he learned that they were from *Awhya*, which he had always pronounced Ohio. The bride was sitting next to him, and this, he decided, was a minor disaster. But at least he had the left rear window seat and could stare out at the passing scenes. The right window seat was occupied by a rather stout merchant who, when asked, simply said that he was "in retail." On the floor, caressed by eight knees, was the teenager who seemed insipid enough, but polite and not talkative. When asked about his discomfort on the floor, he replied with a straight face, "I don't mind it at all. It seems just like a hayride." Somehow this broke the tension and everyone laughed.

In the front seat, two women sat together. One was a middle-aged creature with a blotchy complexion suggesting a skin disease. The other was younger, sexually well endowed, but hiding behind a pair of dark glasses. A perfect stereotype, Keltnor decided; a true Gothic out of the American Dream—before the trip is over, she would certainly regale them with her career in pictures.

As Keltnor was completing his first "sorting out" process, the blotchy-complected woman in the front declared, "Driver, you'll have to stop. I have to go to the bathroom."

Slim sounded amiable enough. "Okay. Everybody holler when they get the urge. But let's all try to go at once so we cut down on stops."

He pulled over at the next roadside café. There was a scramble of bodies trying to get past Mr. "In Retail" who at first decided he would stay in the car. Then, sighing despondently, he murmured, "Well, guess I might as well wring mine out, too." He smelled of liver and onions.

When everyone returned, the two women in front had a mild argument about position. "After you," said one.

"No, you go first."

"I'd rather sit by the window."

"I'm sorry. That's *my* seat. That's how we started."

"Well, that doesn't mean we have to *stay* that way. I'm not going to sit in the middle all the way to Chicago!"

Keltnor rather enjoyed the mood of hostility. It seemed fitting, somehow. Only a few miles out of Los Angeles, and already everyone hated each other with fine impartiality.

Slim, in his deep Texas drawl, suggested that everyone relax. "When we hit the mountains, you'll get real friendly."

"What do you mean?"

"Taking a special route," Slim replied. "For special reasons."

"What reasons?"

No answer.

Keltnor got the point and decided to "help Slim out." "I know that route. That'll make a Christian out of a

Mohammedan." He caught the fear in their glances and in their silence, and wondered what had prompted him to add his own needle to Slim's warning. All he could hear was the sound of Hitler's speech of two months ago. Germany, of course, had finished Poland in a matter of days. The Nazis were ready to devour Europe at a rapid rate. The English were waiting for the blitzkrieg of London to begin. Bookmakers were laying odds that the U.S. would be hit in within a year. Keltnor remembered how bitterly he had laughed that night when Hitler had screamed at him over the radio in the lobby of the Seattle YMCA, how the hysteria in Hitler's voice had scared the hell out of him. And then, because of the absurdity of it all, he had realized that his only defense was to *laugh.* For the past two months he'd been laughing *at* and *with* events, because this was his only defense. He was laughing at everyone in this car now, which explained why he had accentuated Slim's warning.

Slim, however, was puzzled. "What route do you think I'm taking?"

"Never mind. I know." Keltnor began humming Kate Smith's theme song, "When the Moon Comes over the Mountain." The others regarded him oddly, and with stony silence, thinking surely: a real nut in their midst!

"Turn on the radio," someone asked.

"Ain't no radio," Slim replied.

"There is too. I can see it."

"Ain't working very good."

"Turn on the heater."

"That ain't working either."

"What'll we do when we get into the mountains? We'll freeze!"

"I've got blankets," said Slim.

The couple next to Keltnor already had a blanket of their own, which she had bundled around her husband, who seemed to be ill. Keltnor felt the bride's hips, and for a moment it gave him a thrill. But when she spoke in a nasal whine, the titillation ceased.

"I'm Mrs. Ralph Stinson. We're on our honeymoon. We're going back to my husband's family near Canton."

"Oh," said Keltnor.

"Where are you going?"

"Chicago."

"You live in Chicago?"

"I don't know." She looked at him puzzled, as Keltnor thought it over. Where the hell did he live? He decided it was a proper answer and let it go at that.

"Ralph," she scolded her husband, "Don't take all the blanket. Leave some for me. You do that even in bed."

"Yes, dear," Ralph replied, feverish and bored.

Keltnor busied himself with reconstructing the good time he had had with a girl he had met in Seattle. The thought of her gave him an erection. However, Mrs. Stinson would not let him alone.

"I don't trust that driver," she said. "Do you?"

"I certainly don't," Keltnor said, trying to put some fear into his voice. "I think he's carrying a gun."

"Ohmigod! Really?"

"Not sure. Saw a bulge in his pants."

"We were warned about these wildcat trips. They stop for gas and coffee somewhere in the desert. While the passengers are inside, the driver takes off, leaving everyone stranded. It happens all the time."

"Dear, don't talk so silly," Ralph protested.

"I'm not talking silly. They *do* that. I *know* they do! But

I tell you, I'm not going to let that driver out of my sight. Not for a second. Ralph bundle up. You've got a virus. My husband is ill, you know. Very bad virus. It might be pneumonia."

"Too bad."

"Got it a week ago. Day after we got married. Temperature of one-hundred-three. But we decided not to let it spoil our honeymoon, didn't we, dear?"

"I just hope it doesn't turn into pneumonia. That's all we need. Lord, things are so hectic today—with the war in Europe, and all. Do you think we'll go to war?"

"I'm sure we will," Keltnor said.

"Oh, don't say that. That's all we need. Ralph and I saved and saved, waited years to get on our feet before we got married. And no luck. . . . We're going back home to his mother. What will she think of me bringing her son home sick? What kind of wife will she think I am? But our money ran out. We spent too much at Knott's Berry Farm. . . ."

"Dear," interrupted her husband, "why don't you shut up so I can get some sleep?"

Keltnor felt like shaking Ralph's hand. Mrs. Stinson did not stop all at once, however; she merely tapered off. Keltnor agreed with her fears of wildcatting in general, and of Slim in particular. He worried her further by telling her about the altitudes they would encounter in the mountains. This would be dangerous for Ralph's virus, he warned. She had better keep a close eye on her husband.

Facing all these worries and fears, Mrs. Stinson eventually lapsed into fretful silence along with the others. Slim's cigarette burned bright in the darkness. Keltnor could see the stars overhead. The rush of cool damp air signaled the approach of the cruel Mojave. The glare of passing headlights grew less frequent. The general resentment of being thrust together in a crowded car for three long days and nights, though human enough, began to mysteriously subside, giving way to the bond of common experience. They were beginning to feel the mystery of travelers being linked together—sharing the awe and wonder of being impelled forward, held by forces beyond their control. Keltnor felt it, as he always did, when darkness descended and he was moving, thinking, whither goest all past travelers, we shall inexorably follow. All of us, like sheep, unable to change our ultimate destiny in any way, hurtling forward, going somewhere, knowing that we all share the same fate.

Mrs. Stinson sat there, ramrod straight, taking it all in, her thin lips pursed grimly, her hands gripping her purse. She reminded him of a falcon sitting high on a crag looking out over the valley below; a bird of prey, ready to pounce on anything that moved.

The break in the rhythm awakened Keltnor. Crunch of gravel under tires. Cheery welcome of neon sign flickering orange: "E-A-T." He heard tense murmurings between the newlyweds.

"Ralph, I'm not budging from this car. I don't care what you say."

"Don't be silly, dear."

"I'm not being silly. I'm being practical. I'm *not* going to be dumped out here in the Mojave Desert. You can, if you want, but not me."

"I think my fever's worse. I need more aspirin."

"Well, you go inside and get what you want. I'll wait here."

"Okay." His indifference to her concern quite startled

her. Keltnor watched with clinical amusement. Patterns were being formed between then that would shape their marriage in subtle ways. This incident was a classic example.

She pouted: "You mean you'd leave me sitting here in this car all alone?"

"You said you wanted to stay."

Mrs. Stinson ignored what she had said. The skirmish lost, she climbed out of the car and followed him into the café, asking what time it was. Keltnor held the door for the two of them.

"Migod, it's only eleven-fifteen," she said. "It seems like the middle of the night."

"We've got a long ways to go."

"I shudder to think of it. I'm very apprehensive about this trip."

"Dear," said her husband with a forced smile in Keltnor's direction, "I've been married to you only a week and every day you're apprehensive about something."

"But I really am about this."

Keltnor examined the husband's pallor in the yellow light and concluded that he truly was ill. What if everyone caught his bug before they reached Chicago?

The café was filled with truck drivers, their mood loud and raucous. A jukebox blaring away, "Roll Out the Barrel." The mood, one of youth, strength, vitality. But for Keltnor, just now, the mood did not fit. Not with a war coming on. Surprising how people refused to talk about the war. Papers filled with it, radios jammed with news of German successes, Kaltenborn on the air with dire new predictions. But the people, they weren't talking about it.

He observed the blotchy woman—she, too, looked

unwell—sitting alone several stools away. Slim also sat by himself at the far end of the counter, his sombrero tilted back at a jaunty angle, his long, claw-wizened fingers clutching a thick white mug of black coffee. His lean, vacant face looked weather-beaten and carried a sad, rather baffled expression. The teenager who sat on the floor in the rear was also sitting alone, reading a copy of *Liberty* magazine. But the retail merchant was making time with the sexy-looking gal behind the sunglasses. The affectation of the glasses irked Keltnor; nevertheless, he envied the merchant, and decided he would do something about getting better acquainted with her. He felt an itch in his groin and wondered if that girl in Seattle had given him crabs as a going-away present.

He dwelt moodily on his situation: Going home. But in this case, it would only be stopover—until the war started. In the meantime, it would be good—yes, very good—to get back with his cronies again. See how they had changed. He would make it with one of the Genesyk girls, perhaps. Kick things around with the Dombrowski brothers, and with that goofy Irishman, Touhy. He wondered if Touhy still swaggered as much, and if he still was clobbering friend and foe at the slightest provocation. He wondered if the Letter Writer was still living in his fantasy world. Yes, it would be good to see them again, before they scattered into the war.

Mrs. Stinson, next to him, penetrated his reverie with her alarms and fears. She kept a constant eye on Slim. "It isn't that I don't trust people—my problem is I'm too trusting. But think how horrible it would be if we got stranded out here in this desolate place."

"I feel lousy," said Ralph.

She fawned over her husband and felt his brow. "Poor

darling. I wish I could do something to help you. Eat that warm soup. It'll give you strength. We shouldn't have come. But Ralph, it was your idea. It really was, Mr. Keltnor. It was my husband who insisted we come. I wanted to wire for money and take a train. But Ralph, he has too much pride. All day, we waited around that awful place. They told us to be there at ten in the morning. Obviously, they didn't have enough customers, so they kept us waiting. Imagine, stuffing all those people into two cars! I wonder if the second car came right after ours? We were so exasperated. We asked for our money back, but they wouldn't give it to us. So then we were afraid to leave. Ralph went to a picture show while I waited. Then I went to one while Ralph waited. That helped to pass the time. . . ."

Slim began putting on his driving gloves. Mrs. Stinson pinched her husband. "C'mon, let's go. He's trying to sneak out." All the other members of the Watch Slim Club got up also and began filing back to the car. The desert air had turned colder. Slim produced blankets for the front and rear seats. He adjusted his hat, started the motor. "Everyone comfortable?"

A chorus went up: "No!"

"Glad to hear you are."

Laughter.

"Slim, why do you wear that big hat? It blocks our view."

"It also covers my bald head," said Slim.

More laughter. Everyone appreciated that Slim was human. Even had a sense of humor.

"Nothing to see out here anyhow," Slim added. "Listen, we may have a little problem up ahead."

"What? What kind of problem?"

"Next town we come to, they been picking off wildcat buses."

"What will they do to us?"

"Fine us. Maybe put us in the pokey if we don't pay."

Mrs. Stinson gasped and nudged Keltnor. "I knew there'd be funny business. I don't like that *at all!*"

Everyone was galvanized by the remarks. Not a word was spoken as the miles peeled off. Minds turned suspiciously as the lights of the town eventually loomed in the distance. A shakedown? Was Slim in cahoots with the cops?

In a strange reaction, everyone began introducing themselves, as though by so doing, they would better be able to defend themselves against Slim's chicanery. The retail merchant, who said his name was Henderson, asked a question that was on everyone's mind.

"How much will they fine us if we're caught?"

"They're pretty clever," explained Slim. "They first find out how much money everyone's got. Then, they make that the amount of the fine."

"Turn back!" cried Mrs. Stinson. "I want to go back to L.A."

Slim gave no indication that he heard the remark.

Keltnor had to admit that he was as suspicious as the rest. "You let me have the wheel," he suggested. "I'll tear through that burg like we were on fire."

"Would only make it worse," said Slim. "Attract too much attention."

The car was approaching the city limits now. Slim had slowed to a crawl. The teenager complained that they were going too slow. At this speed, surely they would attract attention.

"Can't help it," Slim responded. "Gotta obey the speed

limits."

Suddenly, they heard a horn blasting behind them. Headlights, approaching at a rapid rate, could be seen through the steamed-up rear window. All the windows, in fact, were fogged, and Keltnor had to use his handkerchief to clear the vision on his side.

"Somebody's chasing us! It must be the police," cried Henderson.

"No. It's coming too fast. Pull over." By then, the car was closing fast. It gave a long, chilling blast of its horn, careened around them, and zoomed off in the distance at high speed.

"My God! They almost hit us! Who is it?"

"Must be the police. They must be chasing someone else."

"No," said Slim. "That wasn't a squad car."

"It could have been an unmarked car."

"Might have been. I don't think so."

"Then who was it?"

"Dunno."

Everyone was wrung out by the incident, including Keltnor, who decided that the speeding car had missed them only by inches.

"Might have another wildcatter," Slim said after a moment. There were two ways to make it through the town, he explained: One was to go slow, with extreme caution, hoping not to attract attention. The other was to "make a run for it"; go all out and hope to reach the Arizona state border a few miles beyond, before the California police could catch them. This perhaps was the tactic that the other car was using. As far as he was concerned, it was a bad tactic; one that he had tried without success.

"What happened?" Henderson asked.

"They tried to shoot my tires off."

"Did they succeed?"

"No. I turned off the lights, rammed the gas to the floor, and made a run for the Arizona border. They put a few bullet holes in the body, nicked a passenger in the arm, but we made it."

The women gave a cry. The teenager said, "Wow!" Even Keltnor was impressed. He knew what it was like to be shot at on freight trains. The reaction was always monotonously the same: sphincter-tightening, petrifying fear. He had no particular appetite for any more of it.

They were approaching the center of town now, a clean, deserted main street, flanked by one- and two-story frame buildings, as western as an MGM set.

"Some of you duck down," Slim ordered, "so it looks like we've only got a few in the car. We don't want to attract suspicion."

The Stinsons ducked down on the floor with the teenager, Harold Clifton, who seemed to be enjoying the excitement. This left a rear seat profile of only Keltnor and Henderson. In the front, the blotchy woman, Mrs. Peterson, laid down on the lap of Miss Nash. Keltnor kept wiping his window so he could see. No doubt about it, he felt tense. And yet, it's all so silly, he thought. Why should we be in this ridiculous position? He kept expecting a police car to dart out from a side street. That lone figure in cowboy hat and boots, leaning like Gary Cooper against the streetlight—was he a spotter? The flick of his cigarette butt into the street—was that a signal for the chase to begin? Yet no chase began. No squad car appeared. Nothing happened. The town remained deserted. Now they were safely beyond Main

Street. Keltnor heaved a sigh of relief. Slim maintained a respectable twenty-five miles per hour in the direction of the Arizona border, which he said was "a few miles away." What did that mean—five, ten, fifteen? Why didn't Slim pick up speed now, at least to forty-five? The danger was over.

Suddenly, one of the women in front exclaimed: "There's a car ahead! It looks like a squad car!"

"I think you're right," Slim agreed. This explained his extremely cautious speed through town, thought Keltnor. Good thinking. Even so, the car ahead was moving so slowly it couldn't help but be overtaken by their own speed, which was twenty-five. So Slim did the obvious thing: He slowed to ten miles per hour.

"Turn off your lights," suggested Henderson.

"What for?" Keltnor objected. "They've already seen us in their rear mirror."

"Then let's pass it."

"And give them the chance to tail *us*? Why not stop, turn around, and go back the other way?"

"What good would that do? We're going to Chicago, not back to Los Angeles."

"But there must be another route."

"There isn't any other route, unless we go hundreds of miles out of our way." Slim obviously thought little of any of these suggestions. They were down now to a crawl, barely five miles per hour. Finally, Slim announced his plan: He would pass the other car at a cautious rate of speed. If the other car began tailing them, he would immediately pick up full speed and make a run for the Arizona line.

"Everyone duck down again," Slim ordered.

Questions flew as he passed the other car. "Who is it?" "Squad car, or not?" "How many people in it?"

Slim gave a running description as he passed: A large sedan. No markings. Windows fogged; unable to tell how many passengers inside. Driver seemed to be in civilian clothes. No hat on head . . .

They were ahead of the car now, everyone sitting erect again. Clifton, the teenager, was on his knees, craning his neck to watch the fading headlights through the rear window.

"Uh-oh!" he cried. "I got news for you. That car is *following* us!"

"Pick up speed!"

"Make a run for it!"

"Get moving!"

Slim needed no encouragement. He slammed the gas to the floor. The ancient limousine roared ahead. Sixty . . . sixty-five . . . a moment later the powerful twelve cylinders were doing seventy—as fast as it would go.

"Be careful. We're going too fast!"

"How far is the state line?"

"They're *gaining* on us!"

"Watch for the port of entry," Slim cried. "Two small buildings, one on each side of the road. Somebody may be standing there, trying to flag us down. Hope he gets out of the way in time."

Keltnor hoped so too. He also wondered about the tires on the overloaded old car. He watched the headlights behind them, still gaining, his ear also listening for a siren or worse, the sickening sound of a warning pistol shot. The tension held them rigid. The blotchy woman was crying and near hysteria. Someone told her to shut up. Mrs. Stinson gripped her husband's arm, but otherwise seemed in perfect control of herself.

"There it is!" someone cried. And indeed, it loomed up suddenly, two wooden huts flanked by signs reading, "Arizona—Port of Entry." We're going to make it, Keltnor thought giddily, unless a relay of Arizona state troopers stood waiting to pick up the chase.

They hit the wooden bridge and rumbled over it with a jolting roar that shook its flimsy foundation. Where were the lights? Keltnor wondered. The port of entry was deserted! Was this another trick? An ambush? They passed the two frame huts with a queer, sucking sound.

"We made it!" Slim said calmly, as though this was something he did every day.

A chorus of relieved shouts went up. Then someone shouted in sheer horror: "No! Look! That car is *still* following us!"

Indeed it was, Keltnor realized. He had a sudden urge to go to the bathroom. The other car was not only following, but was gaining on them at an incredible rate of speed. Now it was beside them, passing them, lights blinking, horn roaring, a car filled with passengers waving at them, as though in recognition.

All at once, the truth dawned on everyone. This was *not* a pursuit car. *Not* the police. *Not* a marauder. This was the other wildcat bus, the car that had started out a few minutes after them. It was the same car that had passed them earlier as they had entered the small California border town.

The reaction, now that the danger was past, was one of indescribable relief. Even Slim smiled.

"I was praying in every language I knew," Mrs. Stinson said, "which is only one." Everyone roared, as though the remark were outrageously funny.

"I had to go," said young Clifton. "But I don't anymore." The women shrieked with laughter.

"Personally, I enjoy being frightened to death," said Henderson, the retailer. "It feels so good when it's over."

"Hey, that reminds me of a joke."

"Well, tell it."

"I can't think of it just now."

Every remark brought gales of laughter.

Strange, Keltnor thought, how crises bring people together. All of them were intimate friends now, willing to share their innermost thoughts, indulging in a kind of candor that even lifelong friendships would not produce. Henderson explained that he was in the plumbing supply business in Chicago, and was on a trial separation from his wife. Clifton said he was returning to his aunt in Detroit after having run away. He didn't like the prospect of fighting Germany, but he liked what Hitler had done in Germany, which was to restore "law and order." Mrs. Peterson, with the blotchy skin, said she was returning home to her parents in Brazil, Indiana, because she feared she would never see them again. But she didn't elaborate. Irma Kay Nash, behind the sunglasses, said she was a dancing teacher, had been an owner of a charm school, and occasionally worked in pictures. Frankly, she was traveling in this lowest economy style because she had heard it was fun. Her glasses? "I must wear them. My eyes are very sensitive to light."

Even Slim gave a bit of his background. He was an oil rigger, when he could find the work. In between he wildcatted because he liked being with people.

"You married, Slim?"

"I tried common law a few times," he said laconically. "But living with the same woman month after month doesn't seem to take to me."

Gradually, the conversation shifted from general talk shared with everyone to separate, private conversations. Mrs. Peterson and Miss Nash talked in the front seat. Young Clifton began an earnest conversation with Henderson about his views on life. Ralph Stinson fell asleep. This left Keltnor stuck with Stinson's wife, who confided her fears about what the future would bring.

"I'm not sure I did the right thing in marrying Ralph so soon. Perhaps we should have waited longer. I'll be living with Ralph's folks on a farm outside of Canton. I'm really nervous about it." She bit her lips and continued her confession: "Why am I telling you all this? I shouldn't be talking this way to a total stranger. But maybe that makes it easier—because I don't know you. Does that make sense?"

Keltnor assured her it did.

"If I knew you, I never could talk to you this way."

"I suppose not."

"I just feel sort of . . . lost. I look at my husband sometimes when he's asleep and say to myself: Did I do the right thing? Is this the way I want to spend my life—on a farm near Canton? He's so easygoing; lets me have my own way all the time. He quit college. Probably won't amount to much, except be a farmer like his father. Then I force myself to stop, because if you see people as they really are, not as you'd like them to be, then maybe love goes out the window. Isn't that right?"

"It all depends," said Keltnor, not knowing what else to say. *Poor Ralph*, he thought. The guy is going to be marched up and down like a poodle. But sometimes it worked out better that way. She would dominate their marriage and gain strength from his weakness. In return, she would lavish her strength on him and he would be nurtured by it. *Any* combination could work, he supposed, if two people wanted it to. Looking at the back of Irma Kay Nash's pretty head, Keltnor had an idea.

"Know what I think?"

"What?"

"Your husband will be warmer in the front seat. I'm sure the ladies won't mind changing seats."

"Do you think they would?"

"Of course. We're all in this together, and if someone is ill . . . I'll ask Slim to stop."

"That's very kind of you. But let's wait till we stop for gas and coffee. Ralph is sleeping now."

"Okay." Keltnor settled down, pleased with his idea. Now all he had to do when they stopped and switched seats was to make sure that Miss Nash sat next to him instead of Henderson. And that strange teenager with his strong ideas about law and order sitting on the floor . . . he'd have to make sure that young Clifton kept his hands off Miss Nash's legs.

He dozed off, thinking faintly lascivious thoughts against the background of the throbbing motor, the rhythm and power of its twelve cylinders, and the roars of the wind against the window. A pesky draft came through a crack, and no matter which way he twisted or turned, he could not escape it. Icy fingers reached down his neck. Then to his intense pleasure, the fingers became the fingers of Irma Kay Nash, reaching down, titillating, thrilling him all the way to his groin. Now it seemed Irma's soft body was pressing against his, her generous curves building exquisite desire within him.

He awoke suddenly, due to a sudden lurch of the car. Miss Nash was still in the front seat. Ruth Stinson was asleep next to him, her head on his shoulder, her hand on his leg, and her breast pressing against his arm. He was certain the position was innocent, yet he enjoyed it and did nothing to change it. Instead, he allowed himself to have a full erection. The only intrusion was the conversation between Clifton and Henderson.

He listened as Clifton spoke: Take away the privileged protection that gangsters in America had. Restore law and order. Eliminate corruption. As for the war, the United States should clean up its own house, before meddling in the affairs of other countries. Clifton, Keltnor thought, deserved to be in Hitler's Army.

"If I had capital to invest today," Clifton was saying, "I wouldn't invest it."

"Why not?" Henderson asked.

"Too much risk. You have to fight too many odds. Corrupt politicians. Unions. Gangsters."

"You must be kidding," Henderson replied.

"I'm not kidding," Clifton insisted. "I'd go to Hawaii and live an easy life if I had capital. A man with capital today is a fool to try and create more jobs. The system isn't working as it should."

Henderson sounded frustrated. "Harold," he asked, "where do you get these strange ideas?"

"I think a lot. Read a lot. Listen to Father Coughlin. I also carry a notebook with me. I jot down my thoughts. Some day I'm going to write a book. You take cities. Like Chicago, where you live; Detroit, where I live. These cities are decaying. Hoodlums run them. Why don't we get them out? Look what Mussolini is doing with the Mafia in Sicily. Hitler might be right. Maybe we should create our own Gestapo . . . get a dossier on every crooked politician and mobster and polish them off, one by one. Boy, would I like to serve a cause like that. . . ."

Keltnor was tempted to join the conversation. What a case, he thought. Clifton had the making of a real fanatic.

"I love my country, that's why I am so concerned with its problems," Clifton was saying. "Our problems are not insurmountable if we approach them with cold logic and minds of steel. We have been too soft. If we continue this way, we'll be another Rome burning. Hitler may be more right than we think. . . ." Clifton eventually talked himself out, and Henderson grew too depressed to pursue the conversation.

"What time is it?"

"Two o'clock," replied Clifton. "We have a long ways to go."

"We certainly have," Henderson agreed.

Keltnor was so irked with Clifton that he purposely started a conversation with Henderson, one that excluded the teenager. Why, he asked, was Henderson on such a trip? He was well dressed, obviously successful—why was he traveling in this style? Henderson replied that he was on a pilgrimage; a pilgrimage into the past.

"What the hell does that mean?"

"I took such a trip many years ago. I guess I'm looking for something I lost."

"No good," said Keltnor. "Going back never works out."

"You're probably right."

"Have you gained anything from it?"

Henderson lit a cigarette to give himself time. He wasn't really sure, he finally answered. His voice became a bit wistful as he told his story. He was, indeed, a successful businessman: five flourishing plumbing supply outlets in Chicago. Large home in River Forest. Summer home in Lake Geneva. A Cadillac. Boat. His wife had a Chrysler station wagon. They had no children.

"Every summer, we'd hook my ten-thousand-dollar boat to the Cadillac and pull it to Lake Geneva. My wife would hook a trailer-load of other things to her station wagon and pull that to Lake Geneva. In the fall, we'd pull our things back to River Forest. During the summer, we'd pull more things up to the lake in the trailer. I began to realize that all we were doing was accumulating a lot of things and pulling them back and forth. It seemed idiotic, as though I'd fallen into some kind of trap. . . ."

"So?"

"We sold both homes, both cars, moved into an apartment on Lakeshore Drive. We cut our list of friends in half. We stopped drinking. I got myself an inexpensive sports car. We simplified our scale of living and tried to enrich our lives. You know . . . culturally. Great books. Theater. Concerts. But . . . that didn't help. Things had gone too far."

"What do you mean?"

"Our marriage, which had been deteriorating, got worse. My wife had an affair. I also had one. Finally, we decided on a trial separation. I came out to California to retrace the steps of the past, to see if it would help. I'm taking this trip for the same reason."

Keltnor refrained from asking the obvious question, because from Henderson's manner, it seemed clear that he wasn't getting much out of it. His voice trailed off and the conversation ended in Henderson's limbo of introspection.

Keltnor felt Ruth Stinson's gentle nudge: "I heard that," she said. "What nonsense!"

"What do you mean?"

"Pulling things around. What's the matter with him? Is he ashamed of being rich? That's nothing to be ashamed of. Anybody who would travel this way should have his head examined. He should see a psychiatrist."

"I'm sure he does." Keltnor murmured.

"I'm not ashamed of being poor. Why should anyone be ashamed of being rich?" Keltnor said nothing, realized that Mrs. Stinson obviously did not understand Henderson's problem. Her tirade over, she asked loudly, as if to find out who was awake, "What time is it?"

"Three o'clock," Irma Kay Nash replied.

"Well, I hate to say it, but I've got to go to the bathroom." Slim tugged at his hat, yawned, and said they would soon come to a place where they could "coffee up." "Don't' spare the horses," Mrs. Stinson said. "When you gotta go, you gotta go."

This brought a laugh from both women in the front seat.

"When we stop, would you ladies be kind enough to let my husband and me sit in the front seat? He's sweating bullets. I think his fever is breaking."

"Of course," they answered. "Why didn't you say so? We could have switched sooner."

"I'm not the forward type. I dislike people who are forward. But I don't mind saying, Slim, if we don't stop soon, it's going to be too late!"

This brought much laughter. Young Clifton came awake.

"I heard that. I've gotta go, too."

More laughter.

"Don't!" cried Ruth Stinson. "Don't make me laugh. I can't hold it."

They stopped finally, but not as soon as everyone expected. Nearly an hour passed before Slim found an all-night chili stop in the foothills of the mountains. The cold hit them as soon as they climbed out of the car. Low twenties, with a raw gale-like wind that lashed at their light clothes. The cold changed their personalities; they became subdued, silent, resentful once again. They straightened up and gasped at the frigid winds. Chilled to the bone, they stumbled, half-ran to the door. Ralph, with the blanket around his shoulders, looked like a paleface Indian. *We're like zombies*, Keltnor thought, whereas minutes ago they had been a warm, cozy, intimate group.

At the counter, under the dim light, they ordered and treated each other as strangers. Slim, with most of the trip still ahead of him, was already a fatigued old man. The jaunty sombrero, the leather gauntlet gloves, and lumberjack boots were only a façade masking a burned-out case. A man who had tales to tell, but no longer the desire to tell them.

The hot coffee and hamburgers helped somewhat. Back on the road again, everyone talked for a while, but without noticeable enthusiasm. Their bodies had been fueled, but not their spirits. They remained curiously withdrawn, despite the crying out for answers that the night and the trip brought tantalizingly near. Young Clifton sat swathed in burlap sacks on the floor. Clifton gave Keltnor troublesome thoughts. Too young to be in the army, but if the war lasted long enough, as it surely would, Clifton would be drafted.

And probably make a hell of a soldier, the kind the army liked. After that, how would Clifton turn out? There were not that many years between them; nevertheless, Keltnor felt the gap. How we resent change, he mused; how we try not to recognize it. He thought of Ruth Stinson, who resented Henderson because he was rich and unhappy. She had confided to him earlier that she thought Henderson was lying about trying to recapture the past. If so, what was wrong with that? Everyone had to have his quota of lies to ease the disenchantment of living. Was her sense of propriety, her sense of the essential fitness of things, destroyed because a successful man could be unhappy and confused? What a species we are, he thought—we "superior animals," with our pretensions, hostilities, and aggressions. Here they were, eight total strangers, linked closer than eight intimate friends ever could be, laying bare their dreams, longings, and fears, brought together only by this trip, knowing they were sharing a once-in-a-lifetime experience. Was this a microcosm of the total human experience? Perhaps. Three days from now all of them would go back to their fatuous ways, back to the same old lies, deceits, and pretensions. If only this trip could go on and on, he thought, so we could remain truly human. Was that the reason he had been traveling more than five years—trying to escape reality under the guise of finding it? Was that, after all, what traveling was about?

He cut short his reverie, remembering that Irma Kay Nash was now seated next to him. He had maneuvered that bit rather cleverly. Mrs. Peterson was sitting next to Henderson, undoubtedly telling her life story. Clifton was still on the floor, alone with his thoughts—or was he asleep? Keltnor couldn't tell.

"Tell me about yourself," he said to Miss Nash. She needed no further encouragement.

Her story was a fantasy yarn, yet interesting enough for a first version. She owned a dancing school, she said. It had been highly successful until she had sold it six months ago. She had a home in Beverly Hills, two doors from the home of Mickey Rooney. She played small parts in pictures. Had he seen Loretta Young's latest? In that one she played the part of a waitress. She had loaned her limousine to a friend who had driven it to Chicago a week ago. Now, she was going there to drive it back. Someone had told her that wildcat bus trips were "great fun."

"I'm not so sure I heard right," she added, ruefully.

"Cheer up. We're together, and the trip's only started," Keltnor said, feeling downright lecherous as their thighs touched. He placed his hand on her knee.

"I knew you were going to say that," she smiled. "And take that off my knee."

He didn't move his hand, and she didn't move it either. For that, Keltnor decided she deserved a reward. Her life story was so patently fraudulent that he concocted one of his own: He was a college professor, fully tenured, at an eastern college—yes, it was Ivy League—and because he was searching for a new set of values, he had taken a year's sabbatical to travel around the world. Now, with funds low, he was returning from Hong Kong.

"How wonderful," said Miss Nash, either believing, or artfully going along. "I've been searching, too," she sighed.

"For what?"

"Happiness, of course."

"Forget it. You'll never find it. No one does."

"Don't be cynical."

"I'm a nihilist." He had always liked that word.

"I think people deserve happiness," she said wistfully. "But they can't seem to find it."

"They not only cannot find it, they do not deserve to find it," Keltnor pontificated. Then, Miss Nash said something that gave him a jolt."

"This trip . . . it's so uncomfortable, but . . . I wish it would never end."

"Why?"

"I don't know. Something about it. Haven't you felt it?"

He knew he had to stop playing games now. He admitted that, yes, he had felt it, too.

"What I told you about my life," she said. "None of it's true."

"I know."

She told him the real story. It was a sordid tale of mistakes, sorrows, and persecution by a cruel world filled with male bastards. Two divorces, a child from each marriage. The second husband, a gambler, had thrown acid in her eyes several years ago, and *that* was why she had to wear smoked glasses all the time. She was returning to Chicago where she was being kept by a theatrical agent. She longed only for security, she said. But she knew she would never find it. "I've never demanded much from life. Maybe if I demanded more . . ."

Keltnor could think of nothing to say. Her story was real enough, but so was her thigh. Also her breast, which he felt against his upper arm.

"Move closer," he said. "Relax." She did. His arm curved around her shoulder. The next moment, they were kissing. Her lips were luscious and soft, although a bit chapped from the cold. Her tongue was long and probing.

His other hand worked at her thighs until she shuddered. "Please! Not here. That's enough."

Keltnor, for no reason he could understand, felt guilty. He kissed her differently now, not on the lips, but with a feather light brush of his lips on her cheek, and the lobe of her ear. The mood he felt was that of a lullaby—exquisite tenderness. In that position, they dozed off together.

Keltnor's sleep was dream-filled, yet sound. They were in bed, Irma Kay Nash and himself. She was marveling at his capacity for lovemaking. *You are masterful,* she told him. *You could cure neurotic women everywhere in the world. I will gladly share with you all women, as long as I can watch and see to it that you are appreciated.* Then she was leading him by the hand, down a long, dark, lonely road. It was cold and desolate. No one was there. Except Henderson. Yes, to his surprise, Henderson was there. In fact, they urinated together. Suddenly Miss Nash was gone.

"Where are we?" Henderson asked.

"How the hell do I know," Keltnor answered. "I've never been here before."

"Are you sure?"

"Of course I'm sure."

"Think again. Don't you remember?" Suddenly, it dawned on Keltnor. He recognized, beyond any doubt, that, *yes he had been here before!* Of course! Right here, on this very spot—how many centuries ago? He couldn't tell. The truth startled him, yet he was not frightened. Nothing like it. Only a sense of peace, calm, and the simple recognition of the truth.

"Hurry," Henderson said. "We must get back to the car. The others are waiting for us."

"What car?"

"You know the car. Don't be funny."

"Where are we going?"

"To eternity," Henderson said, and then laughed. "We're going to hell in a handbasket, you and I together."

Keltnor also thought that funny, and laughed.

Keltnor awakened with a start. He had a headache. He was sweating. He always perspired when he fell into a deep sleep, whether he dreamt or not. He felt strangely agitated, unsure of himself and of his whereabouts. Miss Nash was awake beside him, quite composed, smoking a cigarette. *What the hell happened?* Keltnor asked himself. We waited several minutes before gaining the courage to ask the question he knew he had to ask.

"Henderson, tell me something."

"What?"

"Did we stop on the road a while back."

"Sure," said Henderson. "Don't you remember? We made a nature call. Lord, it was cold!"

"Yeah, I do now," said Keltnor, lying.

"You stumbled around like you were half asleep. I had to lead you back to the car." My God, thought Keltnor. So it *had* happened! *Déjà vu! Paramnesia!* He had heard of these things happening, but never to someone as pragmatic as himself.

"What are you sweating about?" Miss Nash asked.

"Not sweating. Feel cold."

"Are you ill?"

"No, I'm all right."

"Maybe you've caught Mr. Stinson's flu."

"Could be . . ." *Paramnesia!* It had really happened to him.

"Hey, it's snowing," someone said.

"Cigarette?" Irma Nash asked.

"Yes, I'd like one."

Mrs. Peterson said, "I'm so cold, I don't think I'll ever get warm again." Henderson put his arm around her shoulder. Clifton was staring up at them from the dark of the floor, his expression intent, quizzical.

"The heat don't work very good," Slim spoke. "I told you that before. I've got it turned up as high as it will go."

"It's blowing cold air, that's what it's doing," complained Ruth Stinson from the front. "I wish you'd turn it off."

"No, don't turn it off," Clifton pleaded. "It's better than nothing."

"What time is it? Where are we?"

"Its near dawn. We're in the mountains now. Some of the most desolate country you'll ever see,' said Slim.

Keltnor suddenly felt better as he realized that Miss Nash had her hand on his cock. He responded with an immediate erection. Back to reality, he thought. Good. To hell with paramnesia. Bring on the damned mountains.

It was snowing hard now.

Dawn came stubbornly because of the blizzard. But there it was, the storm and dawn coming together like twin evil fates, revealing what could have been a bleak side of the moon. Peaks and crags were jutting up and around them on all sides; the road was hugging the steep mountain, winding ever upward, as a maelstrom of wind and snow tugged at and swayed the car. Everyone was awake now, tensely alert, dazed by the sudden onslaught of nature. The windshield wipers slashed impotently against the snow, and frost congealed the windows so that no one could see.

"A real one," Slim was saying. "This is a real one." The wind tore at them in great, savage sheets that seemed almost visible. Ruth Stinson frantically scraped and wiped the frost off Slim's half of the windshield, as the car groped painfully forward through the gray-white waves. Speed: at best, two miles an hour. No chance now of making Salt Lake City by noon.

Stuck there in the white sea, on what had once been a road—and hopefully would remain one—with a precipice beckoning them to the bottom of the valley below. Everyone chilled to the bone. Chapped lips. Eight humans, mummified by cold and terror, each no doubt regretting having left the warmth of Los Angeles.

"More blankets, Slim. For God's sake, why didn't you bring more blankets?"

"Got no more. Sorry."

A clanking sound then as Slim started the motor, after delaying for several minutes.

"What's that?"

"Only the tail pipe," Slim explained after he climbed back in, clotted with white stuff. "Not the motor. Bracket broke. To hell with it. If the tail pipe falls off, let it fall. Muffler, too. Should keep a window cracked, though."

"Why?"

"So we don't get overcome with carbon monoxide."

"Oh Lord."

"To hell with carbon monoxide. You open that window, we'll all freeze to death."

"Should have taken the southern route," said Slim. "Don't know why I listened to them. They said the northern route. Told me I got to make a stop in Cheyenne."

"Why?"

178

No answer from Slim.

Moving forward again now, slowly, torturously, the wind and snow pouring through cracks and crevices never noticed before, creating a weird devil's dervish of flakes dancing inside the car. And outside, the wind continued to howl like the banshees of hell, more forlorn than coyotes, playing havoc on their senses. All of them praying, one way or another, and watching . . . watching . . . The blizzard, it seemed, never would end.

They arrived in Salt Lake City eventually, in the late afternoon. Five hours late. "Blizzard Rages in Wasatch Range" proclaimed the *Rocky Mountain News*. Cars abandoned in drifts. Several lives lost. Six below in the mountains. Two above in Salt Lake. Winds peaking at fifty miles an hour. No letup in sight.

But the storm was streaking in a north-south direction, straight down the Rockies. In the direction of Cheyenne, where they were headed, the weather was abating. High winds and intermittent snow, but no blizzard, and no drifts. Also, it was warmer. Rawlins, their next stop, 304 miles east, was a sultry ten above zero. And in Cheyenne, 168 miles beyond Rawlins, it was a torrid twelve above. These figures were delivered by the cheerful waitress at the Chowder and Chophouse restaurant on the outskirts of Salt Lake City. She kept track of the weather by listening to a western music radio station that was interrupting its program every few minutes.

"You-all look tired," said the waitress.

"We-all is," Mrs. Peterson mimicked.

Moving along the counter, Slim polled the travelers. Did they want to keep on going? Maybe make Rawlins, although

Cheyenne had been their overnight stopping destination. But Cheyenne probably was too much to expect.

"Hell yes, let's go," everyone agreed. They were far enough behind schedule as it was.

"If we get a break in the weather and if the snow lets up as we go east, we might make it to Cheyenne by midnight," Slim predicted. It was ten minutes after three.

"What are we waiting for?" young Clifton asked. The others agreed, and they all headed back to the car.

With food in their stomachs and having thawed out in the restaurant, their mood became euphoric. Ruth Stinson began singing "Springtime in the Rockies" and the others joined in. After that, they sang "Show Me the Way to Go Home," "After the Ball Is Over," and "Trail of the Lonesome Pine," the lyrics of which no one really knew. Then Clifton suggested "Dood-a-lee Do."

"How does it go?"

He responded with his own ribald lyrics:

Please do to me
What you did to Marie
Last Saturday night . . .

This brought laughter from everyone except Ralph Stinson, who seemed to have improved slightly and was getting irascible. He snapped at his wife frequently and objected to everything she suggested. He refused to take any more aspirin. He refused to keep the blanket around his ears. On one occasion, he asked her to do him one favor: "Please shut up and leave me alone!"

The road improved as they threaded their way through the treacherous, winding mountain roads toward Rawlins, Wyoming. The winds, while still strong, were not of gale force. They hit a snowstorm a hundred miles east of Salt Lake City, but it was not severe. However, it delayed them, and now they knew they would be lucky to reach Rawlins by midnight.

To pass the time, Keltnor tried to get them to talk about the war, but no one wanted to talk about it. It was the same reluctance he had noticed throughout the trip. He wondered why.

"We'll never enter the war," Henderson said, as though to dismiss the subject.

"What makes you think so?" Keltnor asked.

"Because we've come of age. We're not as naïve as we were in World War One. We've come a long way since then."

Irma Nash agreed. Keltnor asked the others what they thought.

"I don't really care," said Ruth Stinson. "We're married. By the time they get around to drafting men, we expect to have a baby. I don't think they'll draft fathers."

Clifton gave his opinion: He didn't care what happened; he was too young to be drafted—only fifteen. He was going to get his education, then get a good job, and live his own life. "America first," said Clifton.

Their attitude irked Keltnor, yet he privately envied them. He wanted no part of the war either, but he saw no way the United States could stay out. Sooner or later, America had to be dragged in. He put his arm around Irma Nash as he listened to her whispering "the real story" about Mrs. Peterson, which Ruth Stinson had passed on to her in the restaurant in Salt Lake city. Mrs. Peterson had cancer and was going back to her folks in Indiana, to see them before she died—which wasn't what Mrs. Peterson had told them. Her story was that she had been ill for eight years, in and out of a dozen hospitals. Only recently had her illness been correctly diagnosed. Now that they were treating her properly, she was convinced that she was making a remarkable recovery. Irma and Ruth, however, were convinced that Mrs. Peterson was lying, or did not know the truth. In reality, she was going back to Brazil, Indiana, to die. "She has death written all over her," said Miss Nash. Keltnor thought sardonically how we always think the worst in others. He couldn't get himself interested in this dreary recital, and began toying with Miss Nash's breast.

They reached Rawlins at one in the morning, everyone exhausted and irritable. Slim had the car filled with gas and got out to stretch, while the others went to the bathroom. No one had the slightest desire to go a mile further; yet, each one waited for the other to be the first to make the suggestion that they stay here overnight. Slim was the most fatigued. He was positively groggy.

"Shall we head for Cheyenne?" he asked.

No one spoke.

"Might as well, I suppose."

"Do we have to?" Mrs. Peterson asked. "Is there something magic about Cheyenne?"

"Always like to make the place I aim for," said Slim. "But someone will have to take the wheel for a while. I just can't keep my eyes open any longer."

Harold Clifton volunteered at once. And so did Keltnor.

"You drive, Mr. Keltnor," Ruth Stinson said quickly. "I'd feel better if you drove."

"What's the matter with me?" Clifton asked with petulance. "I'm a good driver. I'm a mechanic, too. I can fix cars."

"You're too young," snapped Ruth. That ended the

matter. Keltnor got behind the wheel, while Henderson adroitly positioned himself next to Miss Nash. Clifton took Henderson's seat so that Slim, with his long legs, could stretch out on the floor. Ruth and Ralph Stinson remained in the front seat.

After a few miles, the newlywed bride broke the silence. "I'm glad you're driving. I feel safer with you."

Keltnor thanked her.

"Besides. I wanted to talk to you."

"About what?"

"Something fishy is going on."

"What do you mean?'

"I was talking to Slim, to help keep him awake. Do you know what?"

He was prepared to hear the dreary, inside life story of Slim. "What?"

"That man has no intention of taking us beyond Cheyenne."

"How do you know?"

"He told me!"

Keltnor was intrigued. "What did he say?"

"I asked him, what about Chicago? He said he doesn't know anything about Chicago. The deal he made with those people in L.A. was to drive us only as far as Cheyenne. But we paid all the way to Chicago, I said. He said, maybe there'd be another car and driver to take us on from there, but that it wasn't his business, and he didn't know anything about it. What do you think of that?"

Keltnor admitted he didn't know what to think.

"He's taking us to a place called the Western Hotel in Cheyenne, and that completes his obligation. Next thing we know, he'll be gone, and there we'll be—*stranded!*"

Slim was asleep in the rear, so the group had a strategy session, as details of Slim's conversation were passed from one to another. A righteous sense of indignation grew, accentuated by the fact that there were seven of them and only one of Slim.

"We mustn't let him out of our sight when we get to that Western Hotel."

"Don't worry," said Clifton. "As soon as we check in, I'll fix this old crate so it'll never run again."

"You can't do that," Henderson said. "We'll need the car in the morning."

"I won't break anything. I'll just liberate a few parts and put 'em in my pocket."

"Someone has to keep an eye on Slim."

"I'll take care of that, too," said Clifton. He confessed that he had insufficient funds to pay for a room; he planned to sleep in the lobby—in that way, he would keep an eye on anyone going in or out of the hotel. Clifton said he liked private investigation work; he had helped an investigator in Detroit and it was a field he was seriously thinking of entering.

Henderson felt admiration for the young man's enthusiasm. But as for sleeping in the lobby—nonsense. If Clifton did not have the price of a room, he would pay for it. "The same goes for anyone else who is . . . short of funds," he added.

Profuse expressions of gratitude came from the others. Ruth Stinson spoke: "We have enough for a room, I guess, but I would like to have a doctor look at Ralph in the morning. He still has chills and a high fever."

"That can be arranged," said Henderson.

Sonofabitch, thought Keltnor. That guy is powerhousing with his dough, which means he'll have a helluva chance of making time with *my* girl back there. He felt trapped. Maybe I'll play poor-mouth and make him pay for my room, too, he thought morosely.

Just then, Slim came awake and asked what time it was and how far to Cheyenne.

"About fifty miles," Keltnor answered.

Now that Slim was awake, the others wasted no time using the strategy that had been decided upon: a stern, no-nonsense confrontation.

"How about it, Slim? What's this story that you're not taking us beyond Cheyenne?"

Slim seemed surprised. "Who told you that?"

"I did!" Ruth Stinson proclaimed self-righteously. "I felt it was my duty to tell them."

Slim grew wary. "Well, it's true. They only paid me to take you as far as Cheyenne."

"But we paid the Travel Bureau for a trip to Chicago. How about that?"

"Don't know nothin' about that. Reckon if they told you that, that's what they'll do."

"With no car? No driver?" Ruth snapped.

"Reckon they'll have another car. Another driver."

This wasn't satisfactory. Everyone turned on Slim now. They called him names, invoked the police, promised irreparable damage to his car. The audacity of it! Who did he think he was? They had him outnumbered. . . .

Slim sat there in confusion, taken back more by the strength of their feelings than by their words.

"Listen," he replied finally, his anger beginning to grow, "I don't lie to people. That's one thing I don't do. I told the truth. Cheyenne was my deal. Forty dollars. That's all I got for this trip. And that covers gas, oil, and wear-and-tear on the car. Ain't hardly enough to cover and pay my food. This trip I blew my muffler and lost my tail pipe. Motor needs tuning bad. Brakes about shot. You think I like working for these starvation wages?"

His words had a directness and simplicity that was affecting—to all but Ruth Stinson who would not be silenced. "I don't care what you say, old man," she went on cruelly. "You're not going to make a fool out of *me!*"

"Not trying to do that, lady," Slim replied. "Told you, I'm an honest man. Never cheated anyone in my life. Guess that's why I'm so poor." He insisted then that Keltnor give him back the wheel, since getting them to Cheyenne was his responsibility. He apologized for having relinquished the job for a few miles.

Keltnor was happy to change so he could get back with Irma Nash. Brusquely, he ordered Henderson to move over and give back his seat

As soon as they were rolling, Keltnor cuddled Irma into his arms and told her that he had a "sensible" proposition to make. There was no sense in the two of them paying for separate rooms when one would suffice; thus they would each save money. In fact, Keltnor added magnanimously, he would pay the entire cost of the room.

Miss Nash smiled sweetly and said, "No."

"Why not?" Keltnor demanded sharply, thinking only that Henderson had beaten him out. "Is it Henderson?"

"Of course not."

"Then what's the problem?"

"What would the others think?"

So that was it! "You mean, if the others weren't with us, you would?"

"Of course," she said.

This utterly feminine reasoning baffled and infuriated him. "I suppose Henderson got in his pitch?"

"Of course," she said.

"What did you say?"

"None of your business."

It is my business, he almost blurted, until he realized that nothing he said now would do any good. He gave up, and sat there sulking the rest of the way.

They reached Cheyenne later than expected. At two in the morning a weary, dispirited group of travelers filed into the third-rate Western Hotel, and signed the register in grim, sullen, almost desperate silence.

Keltnor, because he overslept, arrived late at the crisis the next morning. Everyone was gathered in the lobby except Slim, and they quickly brought him up to date.

The car was gone. Stolen, and Slim had nothing to do with it, explained Clifton, who had followed Slim at dawn to get Slim's reaction when he discovered that the car would not start. "I got the rotor in my pocket, and the coil wire too. There is no way he could ever get the car started. I just wanted to see what he was going to try and do—get his reaction. But . . . the car was *gone!*"

"Where is Slim now?" asked Keltnor.

"At the police station, reporting the theft."

The women were beside themselves with excitement and began interrupting. Ralph Stinson, who looked somewhat better, demanded that everyone quiet down so the story could be told.

"But how can a car be stolen when it has parts missing?" asked Miss Nash.

"Ever hear of a tow truck?" Clifton said sarcastically. "The car must have been towed away."

"But why? Was it parked in a No Parking zone?"

"No. I checked that when I stole the rotor an hour before dawn."

"Then it must be a *stolen* car."

"The worst part," explained Henderson, "is that nobody here at the hotel knows anything about another car and another driver."

"What does Slim say?"

"We haven't seen him. He's still at the police station."

"Yes, that's where he is," Clifton assured him. "I tailed him to the station."

"I hope they lock him up!" Ruth cried. Then an expression of guilt flooded her face and her shoulders sagged. "Maybe it's all my fault."

"What do you mean?"

"Maybe I started it all. I'm the one who reported the car to the police."

"Oh no!" Ralph groaned. "I should have known you'd get into this. What in the hell did you do that for?"

"Because I didn't trust Slim. I called the police and asked them to keep an eye on the car. I gave them the license number and told them where it was parked. I did that last night, from the pay phone here in the lobby, before we went to bed. They were very cooperative."

"But why did you do that?" Clifton demanded. "I told you I'd fix the car so it wouldn't start. Here's the rotor, right here. I bet there isn't another one like it in town."

Keltnor, now that he had the story, was as baffled as the rest. While they were rehashing the mysterious events, he slipped over to the registration desk and asked the clerk which room Miss Nash occupied. Room 219, he was told. "How about Mr. Henderson's room?" "Two-seventeen" said the clerk. His worst fears were realized. Adjoining rooms. Probably with a connecting door. On his way to the community bathroom at the end of the hall of the second floor, he had noticed Irma coming out of a room. On his way back to his own room, 204, he had checked and sure enough, it was room 217. He cursed to himself; but with a stoicism born of long experience in trying to understand the mysterious female race, he resigned himself.

He rejoined the group convened in a corner of the dreary lobby with its cuspidors, straight-backed chairs, pictures of rodeos, and the stuffed head of a bull moose protruding from a wall. He took a seat under the moose and looked at the clock across the room: 8:45.

Suddenly Slim came in the door—as cadaverous-looking as ever, still tired, and very angry.

"Like to find that sonofabitch," he muttered.

"What sonofabitch?" Keltnor asked.

"The sonofabitch who tipped off the police that my car was in Cheyenne."

"Why?"

"The cops reported the license number to the finance company. They had a list, and my number was on it."

"Why does that matter?"

"I'm behind in my payments, that's why. I bought that limo nine months ago, and I'm three months behind in my payments. They towed it away."

"Who? The cops?"

"The finance company. Yeah," said Slim woefully, "someone Judas'd me. Can't believe anyone would want to do that. Who could be that low?"

"Anyone that low should be tarred and feathered," said Ralph glaring grimly at his wife.

"It was a woman," said Slim. "I know that much."

"How do you know?" someone asked.

"The cops told me. Said some woman called in the middle of the night." Ruth concentrated her gaze on the bull moose staring down benignly at them all.

"That ain't all," Slim continued, his anger creating red splotches on his leathery neck. "Some other sonofabitch pulled the wires off my distributor cap, disconnected the battery, let the air out of the two front tires, and stole the rotor!"

"How do you know that?" Clifton asked with feigned innocence.

"The finance company reported that was the condition of the car when they towed it away."

"They're probably lying," Clifton bluffed. "I took a walk early this morning before anyone was up, and the car looked all right to me."

Slim shrugged. "What difference does it make now? Except that they'll pay hell trying to get a rotor for that car in this town."

"If you can get the car back, I bet I could find a rotor to fit that model," said Clifton.

"Where?"

"I don't know. But there must be one in this town. A junkyard maybe."

"What difference does it make?" said Slim, his anger gone now, utterly defeated. "It's their car. Let them have it. They'll have to put a new muffler and tail pipe on. Damn thing burns oil. Motor's about shot. Let 'em have it."

The pall of silence was broken by Ralph, who had a wisp of an idea. "How about the finance company? Can't you make a deal with them?"

"What kind of a deal? I got twenty dollars in my pocket. Talked to the main office in Chicago. Cost me a dollar forty-five to make the damned call. They told me I got to make up three back payments and pay two in advance to get back the car."

"How much does that come to, Slim?" asked Henderson.

Slim looked at a scrap of paper. "Five hundred sixty-two dollars. I ain't seen that much money in a year. Well, you folks might as well start making other plans. Nothing more I can do for you."

"But what about another car? Another driver?"

Slim responded with a faint smile. "Ain't no other car. Ain't no other driver."

"There isn't?"

"Never was. I'm it. I'm the one who's supposed to get you to Chicago. And I was gonna take you, too. But like I say, I got a lousy forty bucks for this trip. Thought I'd try and promote you folks for a little more dough. If you didn't pay, I still was gonna take you. 'Cause I'm an honest man."

"You mean?" asked Keltnor, "if we hadn't paid you more money, you still would have taken us?"

"Of course. Ain't never welched on a deal yet. Sometimes passengers feel sorry for me when they find out how little I get for this wildcatting."

So, here we are, thought Keltnor, all of us, impartially hoist on our own petard. A sad and sorry lot of travelers. What next? He didn't really care. It was really quite amusing, if one had the sense of humor he had recently developed. There were private little conferences going on in various corners of the room. Henderson talking to Irma Kay Nash. Mrs. Peterson talking to Ralph Stinson. Clifton talking to Ruth. All of them obviously asking each other the same question: What do we do now? How much money have you got? What's the cheapest way to get to Chicago from here? Finally, Henderson called for attention:

"Slim, you said the bill is how much? Five hundred sixty-two dollars?"

"That's right. Plus, maybe there is a fine of some sort at the police station. They said it wouldn't be much."

"Where is the police station?"

"Two blocks down the street, and around the corner. Why?"

Henderson smiled. "You folks just stay here. I'm going down there to straighten this matter out so we can all go on to Chicago. I don't care what it takes."

"What do you mean?"

"You heard me. Just be patient. It may take a little while, maybe an hour or two. But I'll handle it. Slim, you stay here. I want to talk with the police alone. If I need you, I'll send for you. And, Clifton, you'd better start looking around town for that rotor you said you could find someplace. We'll need it."

Clifton grinned, patted his pocket, and winked at Henderson. The others watched in open-mouthed amazement and gratitude as Henderson majestically walked out the door.

"What a wonderful man!" cried Mrs. Peterson.

"You mean he's going to pay for the car?"

"Of course he is. That's the kind of man he is. He's going to settle with the police, then make the best deal he can with the finance company."

"Wow!" exclaimed Clifton. "How's that for generosity?"

Even Keltnor grudgingly had to admit that Henderson was showing his true colors. Not to mention making great points with Irma Kay Nash. No wonder she had slept with him last night. Still and all, it was a generous gesture. Henderson probably would have to sign for the car, and trust Slim to pay him back—which had to be the longest shot of the century, considering how little Slim made.

"I just feel awful," Ruth Stinson declared, "for being so suspicious of Mr. Henderson."

"He's a wonderful man," Miss Nash beamed.

"I realize that now," Ruth agreed. "It's just that . . . his story about rediscovering the past . . . I found that hard to believe."

"You shouldn't be so cynical, my dear."

"I know I shouldn't. And I know I am," Ruth said.

"You sure as hell are," Ralph agreed.

The crisis over, everyone now relaxed. Ralph buried his nose in the morning paper. Clifton made notes in his notebook and wrote postcards, the women rehashed the exciting events of the trip. Slim decided he'd go next door and have a cup of coffee.

Keltnor thought that was a good idea—along with scrambled eggs and bacon. Soon, courtesy of Santa Claus Henderson, they would be rolling on to Chicago, the last leg of their journey. It would be a long one. About a thousand miles. He was aching to get back home now, anxious to see his old friends. "Miss Nash," he said, "How about joining Slim and me for a little breakfast?"

"Thank you," she answered. "I've already had mine. Besides, all this excitement has me wilted. I'm going upstairs to lay down for a few minutes."

"Anyone else?" Keltnor asked.

The others said they would be along soon. Mrs. Peterson said she, too, would go to her room to rest. Ralph Stinson sat there staring at the bull moose, pondering the wily ways of fate.

In the coffee shop, Slim, sitting next to Keltnor, stirred his cup slowly and mused aloud. "Looks like my faith in human nature is going to be restored."

"Looks that way," Keltnor admitted.

"If he repays my obligation to that finance company, I'll pay him every cent, if it takes me three years."

"Forget it," said Keltnor.

"Why?"

"He's got the dough. Five hundred bucks probably means no more to him than five cents to you."

"That isn't the point."

"Maybe not. But you can be sure that something will happen to put things back to where they were."

"What do you mean?"

"On balance, human nature doesn't change much. The law of averages simply caught up with you." Slim did not understand, and Keltnor was not in the mood to explain. He was still disgruntled, about Henderson having used his dough to get the inside track with Miss Nash.

Back in the lobby they gathered again, waiting patiently for Henderson to return. And to pass the time they played their own unique version of Confessions.

"Here's your rotor and coil wire, Slim," Clifton blurted out. "I'm the one who took it. And I let the air out of your tires, too. Don't ask me why. I'm just a destructive klepto-maniac, I guess."

Slim did not seem surprised. So much had happened, he had given up trying to understand human behavior. Silently, he took the rotor and coil wire and put them in his pocket.

"I have something to confess, also," said Ruth Stinson. "I'm the one who called the police. I feel terrible about it."

"Why did you do that?" Slim asked.

"I thought you were going to sneak off."

"I figured as much," Slim grunted.

"I'm terribly sorry, Slim. I apologize."

"Forget it."

"I have something to confess, too," Keltnor added. "I slept alone last night, and I feel terrible about it."

Everyone laughed, except Irma Kay Nash, who blushed, and signaled Keltnor with a winsome smile that seemed to say: Don't give up. I really do like you very much. *Or was that his ego talking?*

"And I was trying to promote you for more money," Slim said with a faint smile. "But I done told you that already. I guess none of us got clean hands, to tell the truth about it."

Mrs. Peterson and Miss Nash had no confessions to make. Ralph Stinson said bluntly: "I still feel lousy. But not as bad as I did yesterday. My wife's activities got me so mad, I think it helped knock out my flu."

An hour passed in this manner before the group began to get restless. The women went to their rooms to freshen up and pack their things, for surely Mr. Henderson would be along shortly. Slim and Clifton decided to go to the police station to see how Henderson was progressing, and also to restore the rotor and coil wire to the car.

Ten minutes later, they returned in a state of wild excitement. *"Henderson isn't there!"* cried Clifton to the others in the lobby.

"He never went there," Slim added.

"That's right. The police said no one was there."

"Then, where is he? Where did he go?"

"I don't know. He *disappeared,* it seems."

"Just like that? In thin air? *Impossible!*"

Not impossible at all, Keltnor thought, a bit smugly. The law of averages had simply caught up with Slim sooner than expected. The plain, old-fashioned truth was that Henderson had flown the coop. When Keltnor told the group his opinion they turned on him and violently disagreed.

"I refuse to believe it!" exclaimed Ruth Stinson. "I absolutely refuse to believe it!"

Ralph Stinson said he was not so sure. But Mrs. Peterson refused to believe it, too. Slim said he didn't know what to believe. Clifton said, incongruously, "How am I going to put the rotor on when we can't find the car? The police won't tell us where it is."

"What the hell difference does that make?" said Ralph. "The question is, where's Henderson?"

"And where's Miss Nash?"

"Who?"

"Miss Nash."

"She's up in her room."

"Are you sure?"

Suddenly, they realized that Miss Nash had not come downstairs since the time that the three woman had gone to their rooms to freshen up and pack their things. That had been twenty minutes ago. Keltnor bounded up the stairs and knocked on the door.

No answer.

He turned the knob. It opened.

The room was empty. Bed sheets in disarray. No evidence of personal belongings. It was all becoming very clear—and very simple. There was a fire escape at the end of the hall on the second floor. Miss Nash, right now, was rendezvousing with Henderson, and, no doubt, had in her busy hands the belongings of both.

But *where?* he asked himself. Train station or bus station, whichever had the earliest transportation leaving Cheyenne for Chicago.

He ran down the fire escape, intent on finding out the answer before confronting the rest. He asked the first stranger on the street the directions to the bus and train depots. Five blocks away for the bus depot; three blocks away for the train depot. He ran toward the trains.

As it happened, he didn't have to go all the way. Two blocks away, at a corner, a Greyhound bus appeared and slowed to a stop as it made a left-hand turn. Keltnor jumped up on a fireplug to get a better view of the passengers.

There weren't many. Scarcely a dozen. And sure enough, among them, he recognized Henderson and Irma Kay Nash.

They recognized him too. And they *smiled*! It was the strangest, slyest, most cunning smile he had ever seen. It was filled with an ocean of meaning about the mystery, the comedy, the tragedy, and the chicanery of human behavior.

As the bus moved on, he returned to the Western Hotel to tell everyone what had happened. And that, of course, was a sad thing to have to do. Sad, likewise, to experience; to hear their storm of anger, tears, self-pity, vilification, curses, and wrath at not only the two culprits, but the whole human race.

While the group sat there raving and ranting and pacing the floor and wringing their hands, Keltnor quietly slipped off.

On the highway once again, thumbing it the last leg of the way to Chicago, Keltnor thought, to each his own. Bitter? Not at all. Just one more reaffirmation that this is the way the real world is. What a fitting way to end a trip, he thought with amusement. Not only a trip, but a decade. An era. And perhaps, a very good and honest way to enter the next one.

He reached into his pocket for some chewing tobacco. None there. It was purely force of habit. He had quit that dumb habit months ago. It was a hangover from high school days when every kid had to do something dumb to impress his peers. Then he spit. Again, force of habit. Curious about the color. It was red. Spit again. Still red. This had started a month ago. TB? Maybe. Probably. Gotta find out where that TB sanitarium is in Chicago. They don't charge. All free. Good thing, because TB was growing in this Depression. Kind of scary.

Then came a happy thought. Maybe TB could keep him out of the war. He almost smiled. Always look for the bright side of things, he told himself. Got to keep remembering that. He spat a third time. Didn't even bother to check the color this time.

Strolling down Highway 30 that cold winter's day, he thought about the tumultuous experiences he had had in the past decade—the confused, insecure, paranoid Thirties. What did one learn from experience? He wasn't sure. Except that he had learned about himself, about his country, about the human condition. Enough, hopefully, to endure and survive what was to come. Was hope a part of the recipe for living? Sure it was. The human animal was curiously predisposed toward hope. That was the essential, tragic part of its flawed nature. But, on balance, he guessed he wouldn't want it any other way.

People, he reflected, were as good as travelers can be who intimately share their hopes, dreams, and fears in the dark of night. And as bad, as human as Henderson who left them stranded after his promise of rescue. Why blame Henderson? Maybe he really didn't have the money. Maybe, as Ruth Stinson suspected, he was a phony. What difference did it make? Maybe he had the money but decided he didn't want to spend it to rescue his fellow man. He owed his fellow man nothing, if his heart contained no true message to do so.

So why blame it on Henderson? he mused. That was like blaming the Depression on America, its systems, or its people. Why do we have to place blame *somewhere*? Why not spread it all over—on ourselves, as much as others? We, after all, are the people. We get essentially what we deserve. And the future, with whatever it brings . . . we must take responsibility for that, too.

Maybe this, above all, was what he had learned from the Thirties.

But what would it be like for future generations? Would things always be the same? Can the human condition ever improve? Can man ever learn from his or her mistakes?

For some reason, he remembered the piece he had written in Oregon, sitting on that rock along the highway flanking the insane asylum. He felt his left pocket. The wad of paper was still there.

He pulled it out, straightened the paper, and read:

Oh the land, the land
Tell me about this land
Which is greater indeed
Than all our needs.
The song of it, the smell of it,
The color, the feel, the pulse
Of the wild young seed
That makes it so pregnant
And bursting with destiny.

You catch the sweep,
The sound of it
In the north wind off Lake Michigan
At the Water Tower in Chicago.
Or the west wind that
Gales across the flats of North Platte.

You see it in the reeds
Of the swamps of Mississippi,
In the Swedes and the Meades
And all the odd mixtures
Of colors and creeds.
Still young, thank God,
Confused but learning.

Oh Christ, I tell you, buster,
This land, this America of ours
It's growing,
Racing on like a runaway horse.
And do you know something?
Some day it will catch up with itself.

Then there'll be hell to pay.
But I don't care.
I believe in it, just the way
The man in the Chamber of Commerce says:
The land of opportunity!
Yessirreebob, that's the land for me.
Cause I've seen it!
Oh you America!

When he finished, the words seemed to fade out of focus. He crumpled the paper and threw it in the ditch.

But as soon as he did that, he stopped and cried out: No! He retraced his steps, picked up the paper, stuffed it in his back pocket, and kept on walking.